# Nobby by Edgar Wallace

Richard Horatio Edgar Wallace was born on the 1st April 1875 in Greenwich, London. Leaving school at 12 because of truancy, by the age of fifteen he had experience; selling newspapers, as a worker in a rubber factory, as a shoe shop assistant, as a milk delivery boy and as a ship's cook.

By 1894 he was engaged but broke it off to join the Infantry being posted to South Africa. He also changed his name to Edgar Wallace which he took from Lew Wallace, the author of *Ben-Hur*.

In Cape Town in 1898 he met Rudyard Kipling and was inspired to begin writing. His first collection of ballads, *The Mission that Failed!* was enough of a success that in 1899 he paid his way out of the armed forces in order to turn to writing full time.

By 1904 he had completed his first thriller, *The Four Just Men*. Since nobody would publish it he resorted to setting up his own publishing company which he called Tallis Press.

In 1911 his Congolese stories were published in a collection called *Sanders of the River*, which became a bestseller. He also started his own racing papers, *Bibury's* and *R. E. Walton's Weekly*, eventually buying his own racehorses and losing thousands gambling. A life of exceptionally high income was also mirrored with exceptionally large spending and debts.

Wallace now began to take his career as a fiction writer more seriously, signing with Hodder and Stoughton in 1921. He was marketed as the 'King of Thrillers' and they gave him the trademark image of a trilby, a cigarette holder and a yellow Rolls Royce. He was truly prolific, capable not only of producing a 70,000 word novel in three days but of doing three novels in a row in such a manner. It was estimated that by 1928 one in four books being read was written by Wallace, for alongside his famous thrillers he wrote variously in other genres, including science fiction, non-fiction accounts of WWI which amounted to ten volumes and screen plays. Eventually he would reach the remarkable total of 170 novels, 18 stage plays and 957 short stories.

Wallace became chairman of the Press Club which to this day holds an annual Edgar Wallace Award, rewarding 'excellence in writing'.

Diagnosed with diabetes his health deteriorated and he soon entered a coma and died of his condition and double pneumonia on the 7th of February 1932 in North Maple Drive, Beverly Hills. He was buried near his home in England at Chalklands, Bourne End, in Buckinghamshire.

## Index of Contents

DEDICATION

THE PHILISTINE

Of all the sins that do decide
The place you go to when you die,
The worst of all is wicked pride,
An' no one knows the reason why.
It bein' natural to drink
An' eat an' sleep. It's proper, too,
An' natural for me to think
That I'm a better man than you.

When that I lay me down to sleep
No doubt but what I pray,
For night 'as terrors which I keep
Out of my mind by day.
I have no daylight faith or fear,
Mine is a mid-day pride
But in the night a voice says,
"'Ere—Suppose you went an' died?

"Suppose your heart went wholly wrong,
Or stopped—as well it may
Suppose by night there came along
The Call of Judgment Day?
You, lying down in peace of mind,
Alive, and fairly well,
You would feel sick to wake and find
Your silly self in 'Ell!"

Therefore I say an humble prayer,

Which I will own to be
A slight attemp' to put things square
Between my God an' me
A slight attemp' to rectify
The sinful way I'm in,
An' with my penitence, to buy
Another day of sin.

When that I lay me down to rest,
I put my pride aside
An' pray for them that I like best,
An let the others slide.
An' often—when I keep awake—
I thank Him all I can
That He saw fit to take and make
Of me a soldier man!

That He took me an' set me down
Along with human men
Who live in barracks miles from town,
An' go to bed at ten,
Who sleep an' rise an' drink an' eat—
An' sometimes die likewise—
To certain bugle calls that meet
Occasions that arise.

An' I am thankful I have got
The strength of mind to see
It's wrong to sneer at them who've not
Advantages like me.
An' if I had the time to spare
I often would incline
To pray for them who cannot share
This sinful pride of mine.

Of all the sins that do decide
The place you go to when you die,
The worst of all is wicked pride,
An' no one knows the reason why.
It bein' natural to drink
An' eat an' sleep. It's proper, too,
An' natural for me to think
That I'm a better man than you.

## CHAPTER I

Smithy sat on the canteen table swinging his legs, and all that was best, brightest, and most noble in the First Battalion of the Anchester Regiment sat round listening.

The glow of sunset lingered in the sky, but blue dusk sat on the eastern side of the barrack square; where, in the shade of the tall oaks—those oaks that had waved and rustled just as bravely when Clarendon of the 190th was preparing the regiment for the Peninsular Wars—the low-roofed married quarters twinkled with lights.

A bugle call interrupted the narrative of the raconteur; a sharp, angry, slurred call that sent two of the company at a jog trot to the guard-room.

But the interruption furnished at once a text and an illustration for Private Smith.

He addressed the audience generally, but mainly his remarks were directed toward the only civilian present.

"Bein' married is like bein' a defaulter," he explained, and was so struck with the sagacity of his reasoning chat he repeated it.

"When a soldier breaks out of barracks, or talks in the ranks, or does those things within this Act mentioned," Smithy was quoting the Army Act, "along comes an officer and sez, 'Private What's-your-name, you will be confined to barracks for seven days' an' the poor young feller has to do extra drill an' extra fatigues, an' answers his name regular every half-hour.

"It's very nice breakin' out of barracks," continued Smithy inconsequently, "an' so is courtin', but the end is the same. Up you come before some one or other, an' punishment is as sure as daylight. If a feller was to ask me which I'd prefer—to be married or to go to prison, I'd say 'prison' like a shot; because it's shorter an' not so crowded.'

Here Smithy paused to ruminate.

"You can never trust a woman," he continued bitterly. "A woman is like the bright green birds of paradise you buy in Petticoat Lane—all right till you've had 'em a day or two, and the natural-born sparrer begins to wear through. I'm not talkin' out of the back of my head, as you suggest, Tiny, but from my own blessed experience.

"When the Anchesters went to Dabbington there wasn't a nicer, smarter, or more friendly company on the face of the earth than 'B' Company. Nice respectable fellers they were, more like brothers than comrades. It was 'Lend us a pipe of shag, ole boy,' an' 'Certainly, ole feller,' an' 'Do you mind my borrowin' your best boots to go an' meet my girl in?' an' 'Let me clean 'em for you, ole chap,' till all the rest of the regiment used to come an' look through the winders of our barrack room to see us bein' polite to each other.

"It was the talk o' the battalion; they used to call us the Gentlemanly B's' till a chap from 'G' Company went an' spoilt it by callin' us the 'Pretty Pollies'.

"You don't know Dabbington, do you? It's a little garrison town with seventeen chapels, an' a market day. It wasn't exactly lively. Every year there was two select concerts an' a magic lantern lecture on 'My Visit to Rome' by the curate, but it wasn't exactly dull There was a sort of prejudice against soldiers in some quarters, an' in other quarters there was a feelin' that the soldier ought to be rescued from sin. A feller named Rogers, a young feller with spectacles, used to run a sort of Rescue Home, where the troops could be kept out of the nice, bright, sinful public-houses by bein' given a cup of coffee and last week's Graphic to read in a tin mission-hall. As a matter of fact, the public-houses in Dabbington wasn't so bright or lively, an' when young Mr. Rogers came round barracks an' began talkin' about the arty welcome, come-one, come-all, that was waitin' for us round the comer, Nobby Clark up an' sez We'll be round there to-night.'

"Young Mr. Rogers was highly delighted, an' said if we got there by seven-thirty, we'd be in time for the bright little half-hour service that the proceedin's started with.

"So me an' Nobby turns up soon after eight, an' there was Mr. Rogers waitin' to shake hands an' as pleased as Punch to see us, though a bit disappointed we hadn't come earlier.

"'What have you let us in for?' I sez to Nobby as we walked in after Mr. Rogers.

"'Close thy mouth,' sez Nobby, who always gets religious in a church. We was the only soldiers in the place, an' I felt a bit uncomfortable, but Nobby seemed to enjoy it. There was a lot of civilians present. Nice young ladies, an' young gentlemen in frock coats, an' they all got very friendly. One young gentleman with a very red face sez to Nobby: 'Brother, I extend the hand of friendship to you,' an' Nobby sez, 'Thank you, brother, the same to you.'

"'I suppose,' sez the young gentleman, 'you don't often see bright faces round you?'

"'Not so bright as yours,' sez Nobby, an' the young gentleman looked very 'ard at him.

"Then Mr. Rogers made a speech an' said he welcomed these two young military men, an' hoped they would be the advance guard—he believed that was the military term (applause) of the Army element in Dabbington (Applause).

"So then we played games. There was one game that two of the nicest young ladies knew, an' they offered to teach me an' Nobby. I picked it up at once; it was a silly sort of game, played on a lop-sided draught-board, an' one piece hopped over another piece. But Nobby couldn't seem to learn it at all, an' the two young ladies sat on each side of him, guiding his hand for half an hour, and even then he was still makin' mistakes. By an' by, Mr. Rogers came up to us an' asked Nobby if he could sing. Nobby said he'd got a cold, but he'd do his best, an' everybody started clappin'. One of the nice young ladies went to the piano an' Nobby leant over and hummed the tune to her for about ten minutes. It seemed to me that he kept on hummin' different tunes, but I might have been mistaken.

"I was a bit nervous, for old Nobby only knows three songs, 'Who Wouldn't be a Lodger?' 'All Through Going to Margate on a Sunday,' an' a sentimental song about a girl an' a soldier.

"I tell you I was a bit relieved when be said he couldn't sing without his music, an' promised to come another night.

"I asked Nobby how he'd enjoyed hisself as we was goin' home, an' he said First class, in an absent-minded way. I forgot to tell you that her name was Miss Elder—the girl who taught him to play 'Hoppit,' an' played the piano.

"Next day me an' Nobby went out of barracks an' strolled round town. When we came to a music shop Nobby sez, 'Hold hard, Smithy, let's go in' an' buy a bit of music.'

"'What for?' I sez, amazed.

"'To sing,' sez Nobby.

"'Don't waste your money,' I sez, but Nobby went in, an' I followed. There was a young lady behind the counter; she wore spectacles, too, an' she sez in a voice about the size of an orange pip: 'What can I do for you?'

"'I want a song,' sez Nobby. 'A good religious song with easy words, for about fourpence.'

The young lady shook her head.

"'I'm afraid we haven't got anything at that price,' she sez. 'Nothing under one an' fourpence.'

"'Come away, Nobby,' sez I. ' Don't waste your money.' But Nobby wouldn't come.

"'You ain't got anything that's a bit soiled or second hand, I suppose?' he sez, and the girl said she didn't think she had, but she'd look.

"So she turned over a lot of music, an' every time she turned one over she said 'No' 'an 'I'm afraid not,' an' 'I'm sorry, but I don't think—' in her little voice as big as an orange pip.

"By and by she stopped an' pulled out a sheet of music that was rather sunburnt about the edge.

"'You can have this for fourpence, if it'll suit,' she sez.

"'What's it called?' sez Nobby.

"So she said some name that I couldn't catch.

"'What's that?' sez Nobby, lookin' a bit disappointed.

"'Ora pro nobis,' sez the young lady. It's Latin.'

"Nobby shook his head. 'Give me one in English, please, miss. I haven't talked Latin for years.'

"'But the song's in English,' said the girl. There are only three words in Latin.'

"'How do you say 'em, miss?' asked Nobby, an' the young lady explained.

"'Thanks, I'll take the song,' sez Nobby, brightenin' up; so he paid his fourpence an' we walked back to barracks.

"We went over to the canteen an' found Fatty Morris, the chap that plays first cornet, an' asked his advice about learnin' the music, an' Fatty promised to run over it with Nobby the next day.

"So, sure enough next afternoon we all went down into the back field, me an' Nobby, an' Fatty, an' started.

"First of all Fatty run over the song by hisself, an Nobby practised the words a bit. By the time Fatty had got the song by heart an' had worked in two or three little trembly bits that wasn't in the music, all the chaps in barracks had strolled down to find out who was ill. Nobby pretended not to notice them, but they made him a bit nervous, an' when Fatty said he'd got the music all right, an' that Nobby could go ahead with the words, Nobby turned round to the crowd an' asked 'em what they wanted.

"'We've come to hear the music,' said Spud Murphy, who was one of the fellers. 'What are you goin' to do?'

"'I'm goin' to sing,' seZ Nobby, very short, an' Spud pretended to stagger back, an' all the other chaps got ready to run.

"'Save the women an' children,' sez Spud, foldin' his arms. 'I'll be the last to leave the ship—to every man upon this earth death cometh soon or late, an' how can man die better than—'

"'You close your face, Spud Murphy,' said Nobby, gettin' red. 'Nobody asked you to come here.'

"But Spud took no notice of what Nobby said, an' continued to act the goat, an' there would have been a rough house, only at that minute Corporal Boyle happened to stroll up, an' asked Spud if he was the funny man on duty, an' told him to give the soft-sighing breezes a chance of making theirselves heard. So Spud took the hint an' dried up, an' Nobby, who was gettin' redder an' redder, started to practise.

"Nobby's got a very nice, strong voice, but you could hear the cornet quite plain.

"In a couple o' days he'd got the song off by heart, an' on the last day of the practice every chap in barracks went down into the playin' field to hear him.

"Everybody was very curious to know where Nobby was going to sing, but we kept it dark.

"Spud Murphy started a rumour that it was to be in the Albert Hall—but we kept it dark.

"Then Spud Murphy an' a lot of other chaps—mostly of 'G' Company—'Dirty G,' we call 'em—said they'd foller us about till they found the place, an' for nearly a week me an' Nobby couldn't go out for a walk without twenty or thirty fellers walkin' behind in double rank. Wherever we went, they went. It got a bit monotonous, so I didn't blame Nobby when he slipped out of barracks once or twice without me an' went for a solitary ramble—so he said. Well, one night, off we went to the Soldiers' Rescue Home, an' the young ladies an' gentlemen were highly delighted to see us.

"'I'm much obliged to you,' sez Mr. Rogers, for bringin' your gallant comrades with you,' pointing to Spud Murphy an' about twenty fellers who were standin' at the door, lookin' rather uncomfortable.

"You see, they never suspected that Nobby was goin' to sing at a sort o' church, and they would probably have gone away, only young Mr. Rogers bagged 'em before they had a chance.

"So they all come in, walkin' on tip-toe an' speakin' in whispers; but one of the young ladies—not our one —went down an' talked to 'em an' showed 'em how to play Hoppit.'

"Then Nobby's turn came to sing, an' Miss Elder went to the piano. As a matter of fact, I began to get nervous myself, especially as I saw Spud an' the other fellers sittin' up with a grin. Nobby's voice is good enough, but there's a lot of it, an' what with singin' against a cornet an' singin' in the open air, I expected him to lift the roof off.

"But lo! an' behold! he sang as soft as soft can be, an' I could see that Spud an' the other fellers were disappointed. It was a song about a kid who died in the snow, an' it brought tears into your eyes to hear Nobby sing 'Horror!' in a quavery voice.

"After it was over everybody clapped, but I was lookin' at Spud.

"'Did you see that?' whispers Spud, when Nobby did a bow. 'Did you see that?' he sez, when Nobby closed the young lady's music. 'Did you see that?' he sez fiercely, when Nobby handed the young lady down from the platform. I must confess I was a bit puzzled to know where Nobby got his manners from. But we soon found out. This Miss Elder come along to us by an' by, an' she asked Spud how he liked the song. Spud was a bit put out by her speakin' to him, an' grinned an' twisted his moustache, an' said in a haw-haw voice that it wasn't loud enough.

"'Do you think so, Mr. Spud?' said the young lady, quite surprised. 'Why, I—'

"'His name's Murphy,' interrupted Nobby, who was lookin' rather agitated.

"'I'm sorry, Mr. Murphy; but do you really think so?' the young lady went on. 'Why, when he came—'

"Nobby was very rude, for he interrupted the young lady again.

"'Don't take any notice of what Spud—I mean Murphy—says, miss,' he said; but, somehow, Spud had got an idea, an' instead of takin' offence at what Nobby said, he went on talkin' to the young lady.

"'Yes, miss?' he sez, politely. 'You was sayin' that when Mr. Clark came—'

"And then it came out that Nobby had been goin' to Miss Elder's house to practise his songs in the evening.

"'He's goin' to join the choir,' sez Miss Elder.

"I looked at Nobby, very sad, for now I understood all about his 'solitary rambles.'

"'Joined the choir, has he?' sez Spud. 'Well, miss, I should like to join the choir too'; an' all the other fellers said they'd like to join—all except little Billy Morgan, who was a bit afraid of Nobby, an' didn't like the way be was glarin' at him.

"It's gospel truth," asserted Smith earnestly; "but before the end of the week half the bloomin' regiment applied to join the choir. You see, it came out that there was choir practice on Thursday and refreshments provided, and that all the nice young ladies in town were members. Fourteen men paraded at orderly room, and asked to be allowed to change their religion.

"'What religion do you want?' sez the Colonel to young Jerry Jordan, an' Jerry said he didn't know exactly, but he thought it was the third chapel on the right as you went up the High Street.

"'Next door to the little tobacco shop,' all the other fellers chimed in.

"The Adjutant, who was standin' by, didn't say a word till the Colonel had gone, an then he sez, quiet—

"'What's the little game?' and all the fellers said, one after another, 'Nothing, sir.'

"'What's the attraction?' sez the Adjutant. 'Free drinks?' An' all the fellers said, 'No, sir,' very indignant.

"'What is your present religion?' sez the Adjutant to Jerry.

"'Follow the band, sir,' sez Jerry, meanin' Church of England.

"'And yours?'

"' Methodist, sir,' sez Private Cohen, a young feller from Whitechapel.

"'I'm goin' to find out all about it—fall out!' sez the Adjutant. He found out soon enough, for in a week the regiment was singin' mad. 'F' Company was the bass company, because they wasn't so well fed as the others, an' consequently their voices was rumbly. 'A' Company was the tenor company, because they were mostly fat duty men.* As soon as ever parade was over, chaps used to get together an' start practisin', an' once, some fellers from 'H' got together under our windows at reveille an' sung, 'Awake, awake, put on your strength; put on your beautiful garments.' They got seven days C.B. for creatn' a disturbance in barracks.

*[* Duty men are soldiers with billets: officers' servants, etc.]*

"All this time Nobby was gettin' thicker an' thicker with Miss Elder. She introduced him to her father an' mother an' family, an' Nobby used to go there to tea on Sundays, an' carry the books home after the service. An' Nobby stopped goin' to the canteen, an' sounded his aitches, an' bought a nail-brush. An' when they had choir practice at Miss Elder's house, Nobby would stay behind to help wash up the cups with Miss Elder. Me an' Spud Murphy volunteered to stay behind once, but Nobby wouldn't hear of it. He asked me as a great favour not to queer his pitch, an' told Spud in private that if he ever volunteered again, there'd be trouble.

"'I'm now a good Christian, leadin' the better life,' sez Nobby; 'but if I ever hear you talkin' about stayin' behind to wash up the cups, I'll knock bits off you, you putty-eyed blitherer.'

"So Spud was persuaded to stay away.

"The choir was a big success, although the young fellers at the chapel who resigned sooner than sit next to red-coats got very nasty, an' used to laugh when Nobby sang a solo (by request). I spoke to one of 'em about it, one night after chapel.

"'You look after your singin', my good man,' he sez, very haughty. It was the red-faced young gentleman who welcomed us to the Soldiers' Rescue Home, an' he'd been very cool to me an' Nobby. We was walkin' along a quiet street when I up an' spoke to him.

"'Look here!' he sez, very hot. 'Me an' several other young gentlemen have gone to a lot of trouble to rescue you fellers from sin, an' now you ain't satisfied with bein' rescued, but you must go an' monopolize our young lady friends, an' cold shoulder us out of the choir!' I didn't say anything for a while. 'Blessed feather-bed soldiers, I call you,' he said bitterly. 'Blessed namby-pamby soldiers. I call you!'

"'Me?' I sez.

"'Yes,' he sez, reckless. 'You, if you like.'

"I didn't like to hit him, because I was afraid he'd cry; but I proved that I was no Christian, an' he told me I ought to be ashamed to use such language on a Sunday night.

"Mind you," said Smithy impartially, "I'm not one to run down a soldier because he's a Christian. All these stories you hear about Christians havin' boots thrown at 'em because they say their prayers in the barrack-room is rot. It makes you uncomfortable to see a feller sayin' his prayers in public, an' it makes you feel uncomfortable to hear a feller blaspheme; but it's the same kind of uncomfortableness.

"I chucked up the choir myself, because they found out that I couldn't sing—only eat an' drink at the choir practice, an', to tell you the truth, I was a bit sore with Nobby. So what with hints from Miss Elder about my voice, an' hints from Nobby about my appetite, I gave up goin'. But one day along comes Nobby, seemin' very excited.

"'Come to choir practice to-night, Smithy,' he sez.

"'Thanks,' I sez, rather cold; 'but I've had my tea.'

"'Come along,' sez Nobby; 'there's goin' to be no end of a do to-night.'

"'Thank you, Private Clark,' I sez haughtily; 'but I haven't forgotten your remarks about the currant cake.'

"Anyway, he persuaded me. It seemed that Mrs. Elder was goin' to make some grand announcement to the choir, an' was givin' a sort o' stand-up supper to celebrate it, so I went along.

"Nobby was a bit excited an' a bit mysterious, but I didn't take much notice, an' then he started askin' if he told me something whether I'd keep it dark. So I said 'Yes.' So he said, 'Will you take your dying oath?' I said 'Yes.' So after he told me I was the greatest friend that he had, an' that he'd break my jaw if I ever breathed a syllable, he let out that he was in love. Laugh! I thought I'd break a blood vessel. Nobby got very fierce, an' after sayin' a lot of unnecessary things, he asked me if I thought I was a gentleman, so I said 'No.'

"He'd fallen in love with Miss Elder, an' was goin' to speak to her that night. This sobered me down a bit. 'She's much too good for you, Nobby,' I sez; 'she plays the piano, for one thing.'

"It was a mad sort of idea, but Nobby seemed struck with it. He hadn't said a word to her about it, but he was goin' to take advantage of the party.

"I must say that Mrs. Elder did the thing in style. Cake and thin bread an' butter, and jam. Mr. Elder belongs to the Chapel an' takes the plate round an' keeps a provision shop in the High Street. He was waitin' for us, smilin' and shakin' hands as friendly as possible. Mr. Rogers was there too, but he looked nervous.

"After we'd had a hymn or so, and finished off the grub, Mr. Elder said he'd got a few words to say to his dear young friends. He said there was a time for eatin' an' a time for sleepin', a time for buryin' an' a time for givin' in marriage. Nobby said, 'Hear, hear,' before he could stop hisself, an' then looked out of the window, pretendin' it wasn't him.

"'I have to announce the engagement of my dear daughter'—Nobby sat up straight, with his mouth open—'with our dear young friend and fellow-worker, Mr. Anthony Rogers.'

"I didn't look at Nobby till we got outside.

"We walked along for about a mile before he said a word.

"'That's a woman!' he sez bitterly. 'After what I've done, too! Sat in a bloomin' choir, an' all the time I never once missed sayin' "Amen"'

"He didn't say anything more for a long time, but he seemed to be thinking a lot, and whenever I looked at him he managed to turn his head away. I didn't like to press him, but presently he sez in a queer kind of voice—

"'Washed the bloomin' cups, cut the cake, made the fire burn up, carried her books, an' sang anthems,' he sez after a bit.

"We went into barracks together, an' turned down the road that leads to the canteen."

## CHAPTER II

AUTHORSHIP

"Every man," said Smithy philosophically, "is really three men: There's the man as he is; an' the man as he thinks he is; an' the 'man as he wants you to think he is. We had a feller in our battalion by the name of Moss who was one of those chaps who are always making theirselves out to be worse than they are. He was most celebrated for what he was going to say to the Colonel, whenever he got half a chance.

"'I'll say,' he sez, fierce as anything, 'I'll say, look here—'

"'That'll settle him,' sez Nobby; 'he's only got to look at you, Mossy, to wish he never did. If I was a doctor,' Nobby went on thoughtfully, 'you're the chap I'd employ to stand outside the shop to make people ill.'

"Mossy wasn't a very good lookin' chap, owin' to his beak. Nobby sez that when he was a baby, he must have been carried upside down, an' all the blood rushed to his nose. But what Moss was goin' to tell the Colonel got to be a by-word in the battalion. He was going to give the Colonel the biggest talking to he ever had.

"One day when we was all down in the back field watchin' the ridiculous attempts of 'H' Company to take 'B' Company's number down at football, the Colonel came along with two or three other officers to see the disgustin' exhibition.

"We didn't want to see him just then, because it spoilt what I might call the flow of good fellership.

"Nobby was playin' centre forward for 'B,' an' we was encouragin' him with a few remarks like, 'Go it, Nobby—slosh him, Nobby—tread on him,' an' shoutin' 'foul' when the other feller hit back. It's a fine old English game, is Company football in the Anchesters—catch-as-catch-can. The Colonel came just before half-time, an' whilst the interval was on, an' whilst 'H' was bindin' up their wounds an' the captain of 'H' team was givin' his fellers instructions how they was to trip Nobby up an' accidentally tread on his neck, the Colonel strolled round the field, talkin' to some of the men. He spotted Moss and came over to him.

"'Ha, Moss,' he sez, in that sarcastic manner of his, 'have you been getting into trouble lately?'

"We all stood still with our hearts in our mouths waitin' to hear Mossy dress the Colonel down.

"'No, sir,' sez Moss, as humble as can be.

"'Good,' sez the Colonel; 'keeping away from the drink, eh?'

"'Oh, yes, sir,' sez Moss quite eager, 'oh, yes, sir; thank you kindly, sir. I'm a teetotaller, sir.'

"'Um,' sez the colonel, looking doubtful, 'any complaints to make?'

"'Oh, no, sir,' sez Moss, wrigglin' at the very idea; 'I shouldn't think of such a thing; nothin' further from my thoughts, sir.'

"I tell you, we was all struck of a heap to hear him.

"'Excellent,' sez the Colonel, who's a fatherly old chap, except in action. 'I suppose you thought I treated you harshly when I fined you the other day?'

"'Oh, no, sir,' sez Moss, 'you did quite right, sir; I'm quite ashamed of myself, sir.'

"When the officers had strolled away, I looks at him.

"'Moss,' I sez sadly, 'you're a fine bloomin' Ajax, I don't think.'

"There's lots of fellers in the world like Moss—what Harry Boyd, the horse-racin' chap, calls 'future eventers.' They walk about dreamin' of what they'd have said if they'd thought of it, an' what they'd say if so-an'-so happened. But so-an'-so never does happen, that's the worst of it.

"Old Mossy was sayin' the other night—

"'If I ever come into a million of money, do you know what I'd do?'

"'Buy a new face,' sez Nobby, who's got what I might call a practical mind.

"'Takin' no notice of interruptions, that only shows the ignorance of your bringin' up,' sez Moss, 'I'll go on. If I had a million or so of money—come into it sudden, owing to an uncle that's gone to America dyin' an' leavin' it to me—'

"'Owin' to his bein' off his bloomin' napper,' sez Nobby.

"'I'd buy my discharge from the army,' sez Moss, takin' no notice of Nobby. 'I'd give every feller in barracks a hundred pounds; then I'd have me motor-car come an' fetch me; then I'd go up to the Colonel an' I'd say—'

"'Yes, sir, please, sir; no, sir, please, sir,' sez Nobby very rapidly.

"'I'd say "Look here, old feller,"' sez Moss, ' " you think you're a bit of a lad, I've no doubt, but let me tell you—" '

"'It'd be worth the money,' sez Nobby promptly, 'run along an' find your Uncle Moss, search him for the millions; then show him your face an' frighten him to death.'

"There was a chap of ours named Boyle; well connected he was. He had a grocer's shop on his father's side an' a steam laundry on his mother's side, and from what Boyle said one of his cousins ran a tippin' business in Birmingham, patronized by the nobility an' gentry. Fellers who owned horses used to write to him to see if their horse had a chance, an' if Boyle's cousin said 'No,' why they scratched the horse. What makes me think of Boyle in talkin' about Mossy, they were both dreamers in a manner of speakin', the only difference was that Mossy used to dream about what he was goin' to do, and Boyle of what he had done. Lots of fellers called Boyle a liar, but Nobby sez you've got to make allowances, an' what Boyle was, was an author. Nobby sez that as soon as a feller believes his own lies, an' when he finds how easy one lie leads to another, he's an author, an' there's a lot in it.

"One night last winter, me an' Nobby and a lot of other chaps, was at the regimental coffee shop. Havin' no money, we could not go to the canteen.

"'Let's go down to the coffee shop,' sez Nobby, very disgusted; 'I've a good mind to give up the cussed drink altogether. It makes a man worse than the beast of the field,' he sez, so we all went down to the temperance place. The coffee shop ain't such a bad sort of show. There's a bagatelle board an' newspapers, an' you can always 'chalk-up' a cup of coffee an' a bun, if you're so inclined. The temperance chaps was quite surprised to see us. One of 'em—by the name of Adger—sez, 'What's up—got no money?' An' Nobby sez that we'd plenty of money, but we was seriously thinkin' of turnin' over a new leaf.

"'Drink don't pay,' sez Nobby, highly virtuous, an' walks up to the counter. 'Give us a cup of brown varnish till pay day, Bill.'

"Well, while we was all sittin' round the fire talkin' about the horrible state of the money market. an' wonderin' if we could borrow a couple of bob from Adger to send to Nobby's grandmother, what had the brokers in, the question of liars came up.

"I don't know how the argument rose, but I fancy it was over the question of Nobby's grandmother.

"'Wouldn't that be a lie?' sez a timid young chap of 'H.'

"'No,' sez Nobby very indignantly, 'that would be a piece of authoring.'

"Then he explained how Mossy was an author, an' Boyle was an author, an' nacherally the argument led up to money. In fact, all Nobby's arguments lead up to money. It's generally somebody else's money, but it's money, all the same.

"'What you two chaps ought to do,' sez Nobby to Boyle an' Moss, 'is to put your heads together an' perduce something thick. See what I mean? Mossy could put down the things what he'd do, if the other chap would let him, an' Boyle could put down some of the things what he sez he's done. You could put it into the paper an' make a lot of money out of it.'

"Accordin' to Boyle the things he'd done, an' been, before he joined the army would fill about twenty books as big as the Encyclo-what-d'ye-call-it. If he took a drop to drink an' a feller started singin' 'White Wings,' it used to remind him of the time when he was second mate of a lugger orf the coast of China; an' if a feller sung 'The Miner's Dream of Home,' he used to start cryin' because it called back the days when he was in California at the diamond mines, where he found a nugget of diamond as big as a baby's head. An' it didn't matter what you sung about or talked about, it always reminded Boyle of when he was there. I've seen him perfectly upset by seein' an advertisement in the paper for an engine-driver wanted for Central Africa, because of something it made him think about.

"'There was me, he sez, with tears in his eyes, 'as it might be here. There was me brother Frank—afterwards made a doctor by special licence—an' there was the King of the Central African Cannibals—old Oojy Moojy.'

"'Will you surrender?' sez the cannibal king.

"'Never,' I sez.

"'Very well, then,' sez the cannibal king. 'I admire your pluck, pale-face, but I've got to do my duty,' an' he shouts, 'Walloo, walloo, walloo!' just like that, an' out jumps about a thousand savage cannibals all gnashin' their teeth by numbers.'

"The idea that Mossy and Boyle should write a book sort of caught on. Nobby said that the next day he'd go up an' see the young chap that runs the Anchester Gazette. Sure enough me an' Nobby went the next day, an' the young editor chap asked us into his office.

"He's a very nice chap with spectacles, an' he knows me and Nobby.

"'Hullo,' he sez, 'what's your little game?'

"So Nobby told him about Boyle's an' Mossy's new book. He seemed to like the idea.

"'You tell the chap to come an' see me—the Boyle chap,' he sez; so me an' Nobby went back to barracks, highly pleased with ourselves. Nobby made Boyle put down on a piece of paper that whatever he got from the Anchester Gazette he was to share with us. Boyle saw the editor, an' when he come back to barracks Nobby asked how he'd got on.

"'Fine,' sez Boyle, as proud as a cat with two tails; I told him fifty yarns, an' he had a feller writin' it down in shorthand. He gave me a quid.'

"So we split up the money, an' gave the coffee shop a bye. We was walkin' down town—me an' Nobby—when who should we run up against but the editor. As a matter of fact, he was on the other side of the road; but he smokes a cigar that you couldn't mistake the smell of in a crowd.

"'Ah,' he sez, lookin' at Nobby very hard, 'you're the man I wanted to see.'

"'Oh!' sez Nobby.

"'Yes,' sez the editor, 'I wanted to thank you for sending Boyle to me—his stories are fine.'

"'Yes,' sez Nobby, very satisfied.

"'Especially that one about you,' sez the editor.

"The peaceful smile on Nobby's face sort of rolled off.

"'What one?' sez Nobby.

"'Why,' sez the editor, 'that one, where you and he were in Egypt, and you fell into the Nile an' Boyle rescued you.'

"'Oh, he did, did he?' sez Nobby.

"'Yes; and when you were ungrateful, lifted you by the seat of your trousers an' chucked you back again.'

"'Oh,' sez Nobby, very blank.

"'And a crocodile caught you by the leg an' you cried for help, and Boyle said, "sing to the crocodile an' make him sick."'

"'Excuse me,' sez Nobby, and turns an' walks off to barracks as fast as he could.

"We found Boyle, in the act of tellin' a story about an elephant he killed on the Mississippi.

"'Hold hard,' sez Nobby,' I've got a few words to say to you. What about that yarn you've been tellin' the editor chap about me an' the crocodile?'

"'Oh, that!' sez Boyle, in a light an' airy way, 'that's a row-mance.'

"'A author's a author,' sez Nobby, very stern, 'but when you start authoring about me, you're only a perishin' liar,' he sez."


## CHAPTER III

### PRIVATE CLARK'S WILL

"Nobby Clark went to hospital mainly on account of fruit bein' cheap," explained Private Smithy, of the 1st Anchester Regiment.

"Him an' another chap—a fellow named Beaky, of 'H,' went out into town one day, an' brought back two pound of apples fresh from the orchard.

"Nobby said he bought 'em, an' told the farmer chap who came into barracks an' said he could almost swear it was Nobby that he must have been mistaken.

"'To prove my words,' sez Nobby, very indignant, an' pullin' some money out of his pocket, 'here's tenpence. I went into town with one an' tuppence, an' that's all I've got left.'

"The farmer went away grumblin', an' said he'd shoot any more thievin' soldiers he found in his orchard, an' Nobby said if the farmer chap wasn't careful he'd make him prove his words.

"Nobby was 'ighly delighted with the apples, an' ate most of his share an' half Beaky's, an' the consequence was that next mornin' Nobby was carried orf to hospital, an' the Medical Staff chap said that Nobby hadn't got a boy's chance.

"All the chaps was very sorry to hear about it, especially the sergeant cook, who's very sentimental, an' keeps funeral cards of all his relations stuck up in the cook-house.

"'I'm afraid,' sez the sergeant cook, shakin' his 'ead mournful, 'Nobby's goin' to leave us.' An' I tell you," said Smithy, in a hushed voice, "when I heard him say that, it gave me a bit of a turn, for our sergeant cook's very lucky at predictin' things of that sort.

"I got a message from the hospital that Nobby wanted to see me, so I goes up. an' there was poor old Nobby in a special ward by hisself, an' bein' treated so kindly by the Medical Staff chap that I knew it was serious.

"'Hullo, Smithy,' sez Nobby, an' very weak an' white he looked.

"'Hullo, Nob,' I sez, sadly, 'how goes it?'

"Nobby shook his 'ead with a sad smile. "'I'm afraid I'm booked, Smithy,' he sez.

"' Cheer up,' I sez; but Nobby took no notice, an' didn't speak for a bit.

"'Smithy,' he sez at last, bright'nin' up a bit, 'I think I'll make a will.'

"'What for?' I sez.

"'To leave somethin'.'

"'Don't worry about that,' I sez, tryin' to soothe him. 'You'll leave it, whether you make a will or not.'

"But Nobby wouldn't be put orf, so I got a pen an' a bit of paper an' wrote what Nobby said.

"'Put down that I'm a sound mind an' understandin'.'

"'Everybody knows that, Nobby,' I sez, to cheer him up.

"'Put down I leave all my kit to Private Murphy.'

"'What for?' I sez.

"'They won't fit you, anyway,' sez Nobby.

"'Put down I leave all my money to Smithy.'

"'How much have you got?' I sez.

"'It ain't what I've got,' sez Nobby, 'but what's owed to me.'

"It appears from what Nobby said that 'arf the regiment owed him money. Spud Murphy owned him one pound four an' tuppence, Pug Taylor owned him nine an' a penny, Tiny White owed him seven shillin's— in fact, all the money that was owed to Nobby took up two sheets of paper.

"I noticed, though," Smithy hastened to explain, "that the fellers who owed Nobby money were fellers he wasn't very friendly with.

"At last Nobby signed the will an' gave it to me.

"'Take it,' he sez, 'an' go out an' see if you can get 'old of any of the money these fellers owe to their pore dyin' comrade.' So I shook hands with Nobby an' went back to barracks.

"I put it about that Nobby'd made a will an' told the chaps I was goin' to read it to 'em in the canteen that night, an' there was a big gatherin', because Nobby's a very popular chap.

"I started readin' it, an', when I got to the bit where Nobby left all his kit to Spud Murphy, Spud got very sentimental, an' said Nobby was a honest, straightforward feller, who wouldn't 'urt a fly.'

"Then I got to the part where Nobby left all his money to me, an' all the chaps who knew Nobby hadn't got anything to leave come forward and said Nobby had done the right thing.

"Then I read a bit further, an' gave a list of the fellers who owed Nobby money, an' a sort of silence fell on the crowd, and Billy Mason, who's name wasn't on the list, stepped up, an' said, 'Friends an' comrades all: I hope the chaps who owe money to pore old Nobby will be men enough to pay their debts to our departed comrade'—which was a very nice speech.

"Spud was a bit dazed.

"'Nobby ain't departed yet,' he sez; 'read that little bit again, Smithy.' So I did.

"'One pound four an' tuppence,' sez Spud, agitated. 'I don't owe no one pound four an' tuppence, an' what's more, I ain't goin to pay.'

"All the fellers in the crowd who wasn't on the list shouted 'Shame!' an' Billy Mason, shuttin' his eyes, stepped forward, an' sez, 'Friends an' comrades all: I hope the chaps who owe money to pore old Nobby will come forward like men an' pay their debts to our gallant comrade who fills a soldiers grave.'

"'You shut up!' snapped Spud; 'you don't owe him anything, an' I keep on tellin' you he's not departed, an' he don't fill anything—except hisself with green apples. I ain't goin' to pay!'

"An' some of the other fellers on the list said the same.

"One or two of 'em, though, paid up like gentlemen, an' said they didn't remember borrowin' it, but they supposed it was all right.

"But Spud was wild, an' wilder still next day when it got all over barracks that he was tryin' to rob a dyin' comrade.

"He come to me an' said that before he paid he'd see pore Nobby—he didn't say 'pore Nobby'—to the other end of Hull, but I wouldn't argue with him.

"'You know your own conscience best,' I sez. 'I don't think I'd risk bein' haunted for the sake of a miserable one pound four an' tuppence; an' Spud got very wild, an' went over to the hospital an' asked if him an' Pug Taylor could see Nobby.

"They got permission, an found Nobby lookin' very bad.

"'Look here, Nobby,' sez Spud as soon as he got in the ward, 'what about this money?'

"'What money?' sez Nobby in a tiny, weak, squeaky kind of voice.

"'The money you say I owe you,' sez Spud.

"Nobby groaned.

"'What do you mean by sayin' I owe you money?' sez Spud, very wild.

"Nobby shook his head, very weary.

"'I'm surprised at you, Nobby,' sez Pug Taylor, sorrerful, 'saying I borrered nine shillin's to send to my pore old mother. I ain't got no relations.'

"But Nobby only groaned.

"'You must have been wanderin' in your head,' sez Pug.

"'No, I warn't,' sez Nobby, very quick. 'Don't try to get out of it that way. I was of sound mind an' understanding wasn't I, Smithy?'

"'Never more so,' I sez, prompt.

"'Fancy a man,' sez Spud, 'a man layin' on a bed of sickness, tellin' a lie like that! Where do you expect to go to, Nobby?'

"'Don't worry me, Spud,' sez Nobby; 'don't disturb my last day or so. Pay Smithy what you owe me, an' say no more about it,' an' then Nobby began to groan an' make faces. Spud picks up his cap an' glares at Nobby.

"'Don't you make no mistake, Nobby,' sez Spud; 'I ain't goin' to pay it, whether you 'aunt me or not.'

"'You've got a hard 'art,' sez Nobby, feebly; an' Spud came back to barracks wilder than ever.

"Next day I went up see Nobby.

"He was sittin' up in an arm-chair readin'.

"'Hullo, Smithy,' he sez, 'how much did you collect on the will?'

"'Seven an' fourpence ha'penny,' I sez.

"'Hold on to it,' sez Nobby; 'I shall be out of hospital to-morrow.'"

CHAPTER IV

ON ADVERTISING

"There was a bit in the paper the other day," said Private Smith, "about a regiment bein' bathed once week accordin' to regulations. I don't know whether it's true that it won't wash itself regular, but I do know this, that before our colonel went an' advertised the regiment by sayin' it didn't like soap an' water, he'd shoot hisself.

"There was a feller in ours once who used to dig up bits of Latin and French, an' he had one what said, 'Hot tongs, hot more,'* which meant that people are different nowadays to what they used to be.

[* Autres temps, autres moeurs.]

"I've known the time when colonels used to go swaggerin' up to the War Office pretendin' their regiment was the only real regiment in the army, an' that all the others was likely at any minute to go all into a gallopin' decline as soon as they was asked to do hard work. But nowadays that's all changed. Most of the colonels are 'army reformers.'

"It's a sort of a game. The War Office calls all the colonels together an' sez—

"'Well, gentlemen, I suppose you know the Army's rotten? If you don't you haven't been readin' the papers. Now, I want to know what you chaps have been doin' for your country.'

"Up speaks one gallant old feller—

"'I wrote an article for the Friday Review showin' how all the men are drawn from the criminal classes.'

"'Good,' says the War Office, 'I'll make you a general.'

"Then another hero speaks up—

"'I put a bit in the Times, about their not bein' as good as the German soldiers.'

"'Very good, indeed,' says the War Office. 'I'll put you in charge of the Intelligence Department—because you know a lot about Germans,' it sez.

"'I made a speech at a dog show,' sez another scarred warrior,' I said that British soldiers was naturally dirty, an' wouldn't take baths.'

"'Splendid!' sez the War Office. 'Will you have a V.C. or a pension?'

"'A pension,' sez the hero, quick, 'payable in advance.'

"To be a real Army reformer," Smithy went on, "you've got to start out with the idea that things couldn't be any worse than they are, an' you can't see how they're goin' to be better. Then you'll please both sides, an' get a reputation for bein' a deep thinker. But the great thing is to keep your name in front of the public so that when a war does come along, the newspapers will say, 'We strongly recommend that the foolish an' old-fashioned generals now in the field be recalled, an' Major-General Gass-Hometer, the celebrated author of Should Soldiers Be Disinfected? be immediately placed in command.'

"It don't matter whether you're a fighter so long as you're a writer, an' it don't matter what you write, books or articles, or damnsilly orders, so long as it gets talked about.

"We had a feller in our battalion by the name of Hawkey—one of the nicest chaps you'd meet in a day's march. The only thing about Hawkey that was in any way wrong, was the fact that he was always livin' in a fret an' worry that he was wastin' his opportunities. He used to mark off the days that passed without anything happenin' to him with a big O.

"He was the chap that taught me about the newspapers.

"If you don't get your name into print you might as well be dead,' he sez, an' I must say he got his name in often enough.

"Once he was A Young Soldier Cured of Indigestion by Wilkins' Wafers, once he was A Fighting Soldier Cured of Nervousness by Nappers' Nervo. Another time there was a bit in the paper about him—how he always took a cup of Jeef Buice before goin' on guard. So what with bein' Made A New Man one week, an' being Saved from Death another week, Hawkey had a good time—in fact, he was the most celebrated man in the regiment for a while, an' every bloomin' post brought letters from old ladies askin' him if he could recommend anything for warts.

"Nobby Clark ain't what I might call a jealous feller as a rule, but Hawkey's success got him a bit on the raw, especially as Hawkey began to put on side an' start givin' medical advice on the strength of his cures. So when I saw Nobby thinkin', an' thinkin', very hard one day, I knew he had a scheme.

"He started readin' the newspapers which, as there wasn't any murders goin' on just about then, showed he was hatchin' something.

"Sure enough, about two weeks after, all the London papers came out with a lot of stuff about Nobby, with his photograph. How he suffered for years with Pains in the Head after Drinkin', an' Pains in the Legs after Marchin', an' Pains in the Arms after Carryin' Coal. An' how he always felt tired at night. an' never wanted to get up in the mornin's, but after takin' two bottles of Swink's Tonic he was a New Man.

"As soon as it got round barracks that Nobby was goin' to put himself up against Hawkey in the advertisin' line there was wild excitement. Most of the fellers backed Hawkey.

"'It stands to reason,' sez Spud Murphy, 'that Nobby ain't got harf a chance against Hawkey. Look how well Hawkey's name is known! He's been cured of fits an' cured of dyspepsia, an' cured of pains in the back for years an' years.'

"Hawkey opened the fight next week. There was a long account in the papers of how he was bald from his youth, havin' been born so, but, thanks to one bottle of Hair Jam his hair grew so fast now that it wanted cuttin' every two hours.

"Nobby wasn't a bit downhearted. His account came out in all the London and Manchester papers of how, years ago, he'd broken his neck in three places, but thanks to Malted Embrocation, he was now able to turn his head right round.

"Then Hawkey came out with a bit that started 'Years ago I was worn to a skeleton by fever and wounds. I was so thin that when the sergeant saw me sideways he reported me absent.' An' went on to tell about the benefit he got out of Fattem's Cod Liver Oil.

"Nobby soon replied to that. The papers had columns an' columns headed, 'Obesity in Barracks: Soldier who was about to be invalided out of the Service for Fatness cured by taking Smiler's Shadow Tablets!'

"Every new paper that came out had something about Nobby or Hawkey in it. Nobby's was the best because he showed so much what I might call originality He didn't stick to medicines like Hawkey did, but dodged about.

"Once he appeared in print like this—

"'DEAR SIR, I send you one of your celebrated 7s. 6d. keyless gold watches, what I carried with me through the war. It kept good time, and was so regular in its habits that after a bit I got it to wind itself.—Yours truly,

"'PRIVATE CLARK, 1st Anchester Regiment.'

"Nobby bought the old watch from a feller for sixpence, and by return the Watch Company sent him a new one as a little present.

"Then Nobby wrote about fountain pens, an' boots, an' muscle developers, an' things of that sort, so naturally he got a bit ahead of old Hawkey, who couldn't get out of the medicine way of writin'.

"In fact it was Nobby that scored all along the line, and, what's more, after a little time, he got a jolly sight cleverer at Hawkey's own line of business than Hawkey was hisself—namely, in the patent medicine way.

"In my opinion, the best thing he ever done was how he broke down from brain work an' had to be carried to parade on a stretcher, but three go's of Little Champion Lung Polish re-ju-vern-ated him. That was only one of the long words he used—he was a long time makin' up that letter with the help of a dictionary—'reciprocated' was one, and 'rehabilitated' was another, an' 'revivify' was another. You see he opened the dictionary at 're ' an' never got away from it.

"It was the last one Nobby did as a matter of fact.

"It was gettin' near the furlough season an' soon after this fine letter of Nobby's appeared, the Lung Polish people put it in the paper under the heading: 'A modem Miracle: Soldier's Sad Story of Sickness and Suffering.' Nobby paraded at orderly room with a lot of other chaps for leave of absence.

"The adjutant saw 'em one by one, an' told 'em they could have their passes, or else they couldn't, as the case might be.

"When it came to Nobby's turn the adjutant sez—

"'Oh! Private Clark?'

"'Yes, sir,' sez Nobby.

"'What do you want '

"'A furlough, please, sir,' sez Nobby.

"The adjutant looks at him in amazement.

"'A furlough? ' he sez.

"'Yes, sir,' sez Nobby.

"'What!' sez the adjutant in astonishment; 'go on leave? In your sorry state?'

"'Haven't you got pains in your feet, an' pains in your head?' sez the adjutant.

"'Thanks to Lung Polish—' sez Nobby.

"'Won't you have horrid fits of nerves an' can't sleep at night?' sez the adjutant, who appeared to have been readin' the papers.

"'I used to,' sez Nobby, 'but thanks to Bright's Nerve Pills, I'm—'

"'An', sez the adjutant, 'am I right in believin' that you suffer from shortness of breath and palpitation?'

"'Years ago,' sez Nobby, very agitated, I used to, but, thanks to Bilker's Breath Beans, I am now a new—'

"The adjutant shook his head.

"'No,' he sez; 'I can't give a furlough. I can't let you loose on the world to spread all those diseases among innocent people. I want you here—under my eye,' he sez, so that if the worst comes to the worst we can bury you with military honours,' he sez."

## CHAPTER V

ON PROMOTION

"Fellers who got on in the world," said Smithy sagely, "don't give themselves airs as a rule. It's the fellers that think they've got on. Me an' Nobby went to a 'do' in the town the other night. It was a lecture business with a magic lantern about Niagara Falls. The chap who gave the lecture was the heac reporter on the Wigshire Chronicle and Anchester County Gazette.

"From what I could hear, he got a free pass to Canada on some ship or other. He was there two weeks, an' what he don't know about Canada now ain't worth knowin'. A young chap who sat next to me an' Nobby said he was a decent feller before he went, but since he's come back, his head's so big that he has had to have a bit let into his hat.

"I've known fellers who've got on to such an extent that they don't really know how much they owe. An' do they give themselves airs? Not a bit. It's 'Have a drink, Smithy,' an' 'Put it down to me, miss,' just as friendly as possible. An' it ain't always what a man becomes that makes him hefty-headed, it's what he dreams of becomin'. When a feller's had a good word from the Colonel, an' walks about barracks seein' hisself with the sergeant-major's gold crown on his sleeve, he's a big sight more cocky than he is when the bloomin' warrant comes along.

"My experience is that a chap who's a private is a perfect little gentleman till some one gives him a stripe an makes him a lance-corporal. If he's got anything bad in him that's the time it comes out. Between the officer an' the man there ain't any middle-grades really. Non-commissioned officers I've never had no use for. They're mostly chaps who've polished up their school-board education to get out of the hard work that a Tommy has got to do.

"So when I see a nice, bright young feller suddenly give up playin' the goat, an' wearin' a worried, don't-come-near-me look, I know he's doomed for the stripe, and cut him off my visiting list, so to speak. But the most 'orrid thing that ever happened come about three weeks ago. On that very day I sez to Nobby—

"'Comin' down town to-night, Nob?'

"'No,' sez Nobby, quick and short.

"I looks at him for a bit, for there was something is his eye I didn't like.

"'Why not?' I sez.

"'Never mind why not,' he sez, as short as ever.

"'Got no money?' I sez.

"'Never Mind,' he sez.

"'Are you a prisoner or anything?' I sez anxiously

"'Never mind,' he sez.

Then the 'orrid truth broke over me.

"'Nobby,' I gasps, 'Nobby, they ain't goin' to make corporal of you, are they?'

"'They are,' he sez and stalks away.

"I tell you, I was upset something awful. Me an' old Nobby have been pals for years, an I never thought it would come to this. Now I understood a lot. Why Nobby wouldn't join me and Swank Roberts when we went down town to clear out the Peacock. Why Nobby kept away from the canteen for hours at a time.

"It was all over barracks before long that Nobby was goin' to get promotion, an' fellers come from all parts to look at Nobby to see what a corporal looked like before he was born. Nobby took no notice, sittin' on his bed-cot pretending to read Every Soldier's Guide to Promotion, an' the fellers who come in one by one to ask him if it was true got a short answer.

"'I asked you a civil question,' sez Spud Murphy.

"'An' I've give you a civil answer,' snaps Nobby, still pretending to read his book.

"'You might call it civil,' sez Spud, 'but when I tell a chap to go to where you told me to go to, I don't reckon I'm bein' polite.'

"Nobby said nothing.

"'Is it true,' sez Spud, 'that you're going to be a corporal?'

"'It is,' sez Nobby. 'I've told you once.'

"'Well, all I can say,' sez Spud, very gloomy, is that the Army's goin' to the dogs. What are they goin' to make you a corporal for—your good looks?'

"Nobby got wilder an' wilder, but said nothing.

"'Have they run short of soldiers?' sez Spud aggravatingly.

"Nobby got up quick, and Spud scooted.

"Pug Wilson come in some time after.

"'Hello, Nobby,' sez Pug sorrowfully, 'so they've caught you, have they?'

"'Whatcher mean?' sez Nobby, very fierce.

"'Ain't it true, then?' sez Pug anxiously, 'or has some one been tellin' lies about your being made corporal?'

"'Of course it's true,' sez Nobby.

"'Pore old Nobby,' sez Pug, wipin' his eyes, and walked sadly away.

"Nobby was very sore at the way chaps went on.

"'Look here, Smithy,' he sez, 'when I'm a corporal I'll teach these fellers to talk to their superior,' he sez.

"'A fat lot you'll do,' I sez. 'You'll be hitting somebody an' losing your stripe before you've had it a week.'

"Two mornings afterwards it came out in orders that our bold Nobby was to get the 'dog's leg,'* and the square wasn't big enough to hold Nobby as he walked across to the canteen.

*[* So called from the shape of the corporal's chevron.]*

"I met him half-way over.

"'Hello, Nobby,' I sez.

"'Corporal Clark, if you please,' sez Nobby, hoity-toitily.

"'Never mind your bloomin' title,' I sez, 'are you going to wet the stripe?'

"Nobby waved his hand in his grand way.

"'I don't drink with privates,' he sez, 'only with men of me own rank,' an' he turned into the corporals' room.

"When I got into the canteen I was so knocked over by Nobby's disgusting behaviour that I drank out of the first pot I could find.

"'Hold hard, Smithy,' sez Spud. That's my beer when you've done with it.'

"'Never mind about your beer,' I sez bitterly, 'I've lost a pal what's turned into a serpent.'

"We had a long talk about Nobby's promotion. It was a sort of meeting like Nobby used to have when he was respectable.

"'I can't understand Nobby taking the stripe,' sez Pug. 'Where's he going to get his money from—corporals ain't allowed to swindle nobody.'

"The end of our discussion was that corporal or no corporal, Nobby had to be taken down a peg or two.

"Next morning, there was Nobby on parade in the corporals' rank, a-twisting his moustache and frowning like anything.

He hadn't got many orders to give, but he managed to get in a few remarks, such as, 'Now then, Wilson, look to your front,' an' 'Stop talking there,' an' 'Don't scratch your nose in the ranks, Smithy,' till I felt like turning round and smacking him in the eye.

"When we got back to the barrack-room the fun began. We were all in before Nobby and waited. By and by in came his nibs, and Spud Murphy shouted, 'T'shun!' and we all stood to attention. Nobby got red, and frowned worse than ever.

"'None of your cheek,' he sez.

"'No, sir,' sez Spud, saluting.

"'Look here, Murphy,' sez Nobby, very hot, 'don't you come your funny games with me, or I'll give you a wipe—I mean I'll put you in the guard-room.

"'Yes, sir,' sez Spud, saluting again.

"'And don't you call me "sir,"' sez Nobby very fierce. 'Call me corporal, you putty-faced—I mean you disrespectful feller.'

"Just then Pug came up and saluted.

"Any orders, Colonel,' he sez, saluting.

"Nobby was choking wild. You see, he was too much of a private to sneak, and he wasn't enough of a corporal to do the N.C.O. act.

We made his blooming life a misery for the next two days. If any of us met him when nobody was about, we used to salute him, Spud went down on his knees once an' tapped his head on the ground as Nobby passed.

"'Get up, you perishing recruit,' sez Nobby, 'or I'll put you in the guard-room.'

"But Spud still knelt, sayin', 'Hail, hail, great chief,' and things like that, till Nobby, looking round to see if anybody was in sight, took a fine drop kick at him.

"That rather upset the saluting business, but Vaney, who picked up a little bit of foreign language when he was on the motor-bus, started the 'Mong.' It appears, from what Vaney sez—and its probably a lie— in the French Army, when a private talks to the colonel or the company officer, he sez 'Mong.'

"Nobby told Vaney to do something one morning—Vaney's just been transferred to our company—and Vaney sez, 'Wee, wee, mong Colonel.'

"'What's that?' sez Nobby quick, so Vaney repeated it.

"'I want none of your cheek,' sez Nobby.

"'That ain't cheek,' sez Vaney.

"'What is it, then?' sez Nobby, who didn't know more than the man in the moon.

"'It's French,' sez Vaney.

"'Well, don't do it,' sez Nobby sternly.

"The 'mong' business was a great success. We monged 'Nobby till he nearly cried.

"'Smithy,' he sez to me one day, very solemn, if I have much more of this I shall do something pretty bad.'

"'Will you, mong Nobby?' I sez.

"'Yes, I will, mong fathead,' he snaps, and went away.

"I've always said about Nobby that he's got second-sight. He sez so hisself; in fact, when he was a little boy he had to wear spectacles for it. So when he said that something was going to happen, I knew it was coming true. It came about in an unexpected way.

"Me and Pug Wilson was down town one night. It was pay night, and Saturday night, too, and there was trouble in the blooming air. Just before we left barracks we had to call at the guard-room to get our passes. While we was there in came the Provost Corporal and said that Billy Mason was in town drinking like a fish. So the sergeant of the guard passed the word and got down the biggest pair of handcuffs he could find, and unlocked a cell door all ready for Billy. In the town we passed the picket, looking sad, and Pug said to me—

"'Smithy, I smell blood.' And I could smell it. too.

"It's a rum thing how affairs came about. Me and Pug passed a pleasant evening doing nothing, and we was coming back, talking about what a rotten place Anchester was, with the pubs closing at ten, when we heard the picket coming toward us at the double. As they went running past I saw that Nobby was in charge, and one of the chaps called out, 'Billy's got a rough house at the Phoenix.'

So me and Pug went back to see the fun. There was a little crowd outside the public, and inside we could hear Billy's voice and broken glass.

"Nobby pushed through the crowd, and I went into the bar with the picket. Billy, with his tunic off, was at the other end of the bar-room with a chair in his hand.

"'Hello, Nobby,' he sez through his teeth, an' I could see he had one of his mad fits on.

"'Hello, Billy,' sez Nobby quietly; 'come out of this, old son.'

"'What are you going to do?'

"'Put you in the clink,' sez Nobby.

"'How many of you?' sez Billy, gettin' a grip of the chair.

"'Put that chair down, an I'll do it myself,' sez Nobby, who is a rare feller for meetin' trouble half-way.

"Then before he knew what was going to happen, Bill dropped the chair, and landing out caught Nobby a whack on the jaw that floored him, It's serious business to strike a corporal, an' when Billy saw what he'd done, it sobered him,

"As Nobby picked himself up, there was a stir at the doorway, and the Provost Sergeant pushed his way through.

"'Make that man a prisoner,' sez Nobby to the picket as quick as anything, and the picket closed round Billy, who was as quiet as a lamb.

"'Hello,' sez the Police Sergeant; 'what's this—did this man strike you, Corporal Clark?'

"'No,' sez Nobby.

"'What's that mark on your face?'

"'A birthmark,' sez Nobby, quick as lightning.

"When Billy came up at the orderly room he got ten days, an' the Colonel said that if he's struck Nobby he'd have put him back for a Court Martial. But Nobby swore and swore that Billy didn't lift his hands. After Billy got his dose, Nobby went into the Colonel's office

"At dinner-time, when we was all together in the canteen, talking about Nobby an' saying what a decent chap he was, in he walked.

"Spud was the first to do the handsome. He ups with his pot an' handed it over.

"'Here you are, Corporal,' he sez 'drink hearty, an' let by-gones be by-gones.'

"Nobby took the pot.

"'Not so much of the Corporal,' he sez, and then I saw his stripe had gone. 'I've given it up. Private's good enough for me. I like a rank where, if a feller hits me, I can hit him back.'"

## CHAPTER VI

NO. 2 MAGAZINE

No record of prior publication under this title found

"Lots of fellows go home for Christmas, but lots more stay in barracks an' enjoy themselves," said Private Smith, who is spending a few days with me just now, "After all, going home for Christmas ain't much catch unless you've got a lot of pals with you. An uncle of mine asked me home two years ago. He said he'd come into a lot of money and wanted to do me well, but the feller the money belonged to found him out, and I only see poor Uncle Tim now on visiting days. He's in what Nobby calls the Civil Service.

"Give me barracks at Christmas time. There ain't a happier, light-hearteder lot of fellers than 'B' Company on Christmas Day, when everything's free, drinks included. Last year was the most excitin' Christmas we's ever had, more especially because of our pantomime what Nobby Clark got up. ' The Babes in the Wood, or Princess Blue Bell.'

"It was all Nobby's idea, and he went an' saw the Adjutant about it, and the Adjutant gave permission. We rigged the library up just like a real, first-class London theatre, and you wouldn't have been able to tell the difference. Real limelight, a real band in front, and sawdust on the floor, and armchairs for the officers—it was fine.

"We thought of getting real young ladies to play the parts, but Nobby said that that was carrying the thing a bit too far, so we made Nobby play the part of the Fairy Queen, and Tiny White and Big Harvey was the two babes in the wood. Nobby got a feller named Ginger, who makes poetry, to help to write the pantomime. Ginger's the chap who wrote that bit about the wreck of the Birkenhead. I forget how it goes, but the first verse starts—

O, Comrades bold, come gather round,
And I will tell to thee,
A story of a gallant deed
Upon the briny sea.

"It's a fine poem, and I wonder somebody hasn't took it up an' put it in the papers. Well, from what Nobby sez, all pantomimes are writ in verse, and the way him and Ginger wrote that blooming panto was a marvel. The first scene was the 'Lower Regions.' Nobby sez all good pantomimes start in hell an' end nowhere.

"The Demon King was a chap named Jaggers, and he had to start—

O, comrades bold, come gather round

And listen to my awful sound.

"You see, Ginger can't write anything unless it starts 'O, comrades bold,' it's a sort of habit.

"Nobby had hard work making the chaps remember the bits they had to say. Spud Murphy was a sort of fairy godmother, and his bit went—

O, comrades bold, you see in me

A little fairy gay and free.

But Spud couldn't think what came after that, and Nobby used to get so wild that I thought he'd have a stroke.

"'Spud,' he sez, very solemn, 'if I've told you once I've told you six times that you've got to say to me—

I love you, little fairy queen,

You are the best I've ever seen.

And if I have to tell you again I'll give you a slosh in the neck.'

"What with one thing and another the rehearsals nearly killed Nobby. Two nights before Christmas the whole bloomin' show was upset by the Two Babes bein' put in the guard-room for fightin' a policeman in town. But the worst thing of all happened on Christmas Eve.

"Me an' Nobby had been havin' a last rehearsal, an' the play went fine. All except the demon king part. The chap who played that was a young feller named Jaggers, as I told you before. I could never quite make him out, He had a trick of lookin' the other way when you happened to be talking to him; he never looked you straight in the face. He was only a recruit in a manner of speakin', havin' been in the regiment a year, and bein' a quiet feller, with a bad temper—he got perfectly wild when he was upset—nobody said much to him. Nobby put him in the play because he looked like a demon king at times. That night, at rehearsal, Jaggers was very peculiar. He said lots of things that wasn't in the play, an' in parts he got very excited. I was quite astonished when Nobby didn't say anything to him, but just answered him as polite and patient as anything. By an' bye, I saw Nobby talkin' to him on the quiet, an' when he had finished Nobby came straight across to me.

"'Smithy,' he sez, as earnest as anything, 'cut across to the hospital an' tell the orderly on duty that something's wrong with Jaggers.'

"'What's the game?' I sez, for I know Nobby is a rare feller for pulling your leg.

"'Here, wait a bit,' sez Nobby, an' wrote down something on a paper, 'give this to the chap in charge.'

"I could see that Nobby wasn't jokin', so I slipped off as fast as I could nip, an' got to the hospital just as the doctor was leavin' after his night visit.

"I handed the paper to the orderly.

"'What's that?' sez the officer, and the orderly handed it over. The doctor read it, an' I could see by the way he frowned that something was up.

"'Four orderlies and a stretcher,' he sez, sharp, 'an' bring along some stout straps—go back to the library, Smith.'

"I was as mystry-fied as could be, but when I got into the library I could see there was trouble.

"All the fellers were standin' in the middle of the room in their dresses—except Nobby, who bein' a sort of manager was only in his uniform. But what held me was Jaggers. He was standin' in front of Nobby, with a long knife in his hand an' his eyes were glaring something shockin'. Nobby was as cool as a cucumber, which is more than I should have been, for Jaggers, in his demon dress, was a gashly sight.

"He was shoutin' when I came in.

"'I know you!' he was sayin' to Nobby, 'you're the man who has been trying to ruin me!'

"'You're mistakin' me,' sez Nobby, very mildly for 'for my brother, who's very much like me.'

."'You Lie!' howls Jaggers, wavin' his knife about. 'You're the man, an' by—'

"Nobby was gradually edgin' round till he got Daggers with his back to the door.

"If ever there was mad murder in a chap's face it was in Jaggers', and though I didn't like the knife a bit, I steps up to Nobby's side, an 'sez—

"'Hold hard, Jaggers ; you're makin' a bit of an error—'

"He turned on me like a devil.

"'You!' he sez, an' he tightened his grip on the knife 'you're the other villain—'

"Over his shoulders I saw the four men of the medical staff in the doorway, an' though I ain't no friend of the Poultice Wallahs, I blessed the sight of their little red crosses. They were on Jaggers in the minute, the knife was out of his hand, and he lay helpless on the door before you could count two, They can handle a man can the medical staff when it comes to a pinch, an' the way they strapped Jaggers to a stretcher was the neatest thing I've ever seen done.

"From what the doctor told Nobby, Jaggers was a natural born lunatic, an' how he got into the army nobody knows. But Jaggers goin' mad didn't upset the show. It takes more than a little thing like that to put Nobby out. It was what followed. For in half an hour, round came the orderly sergeants warning all sorts of chaps for guard. There had to be a double guard for Jaggers, who was marked 'dangerous.' About that time—we was stationed in a garrison town—the guard and piquets came pretty heavy on the men, an' as soon as I heard about the extra one, I knew where me and Nobby would spend our Christmas Day.

"Sure enough, we was for it. No. 2 Magazine, the most horrible bloomin' post in the garrison. A lonely stone buildin', on the top of a hill, miles away from everywhere, an' on the edge of the marsh.

"The only comfort was that it was a double guard, two men at a time, an' I knew that me an' Nobby would be together, It was snowin' a bit when we paraded on Christmas mornin'.

"'This is a nice happy Christmas, I don't think,' sez Nobby bitterly; 'an' me who was goin' to be a fairy queen.'

"Pug Wilson was paradin', too.

"'I'd sooner have your job than mine,' he sez, 'hospital guard over poor old Jaggers, an' him carryin' on something awful.'

"Spud Murphy was standin' at the gate as we marched out.

"'A happy Christmas, Bluebell dear; it only comes but once a year,' he sez, sayin' his lines with a grin.

"'When I get back,' sez Nobby, through his teeth. 'I'll take Spud by the neck, an' bash his fat head—'

"'Silence in the ranks,' sez the sergeant.

"It turned out to be a most perfectly rotten day. It snowed, an' snowed, an' snowed, an' the wind that came sweepin' round the magazine nearly cut you in two. Me an' Nobby was second relief, twelve till two and six till eight.

"We stood together in the afternoon, lookin' towards the barracks. They are about two miles away from the magazine, an' the guard-room's about a half a mile away.

"'To think,' sez Nobby, 'that me an' you are stuck here, doing sentry go, whilst a mud-faced Cockney plasterer like Spud Murphy is drinkin' free beer in barracks—why, it's enough to make a chap go cracked like poor old Jaggers.'

"That afternoon a feller who came up from barracks said Jaggers was better, but was still in the padded cell, an' nobody had gone in to him yet. It was a miserable day.

"When we was 'off' we sat in front of the guard room fire an' told yarns. Bill Hatchett told a yarn about a ghost in India, an' Nobby told a yarn about a chap who used to walk about barracks at Christmas time with his 'ead under his arm, an' another feller told a tale about a ghost he saw once.

"'When you've all finished tellin' lies,' I sez, 'you might wake me up, I'm goin' to snatch a sleep.'

'The corporal of the guard woke me an' Nobby just before twelve, an' I've never felt less inclined for guard. It was snowin' hard when we got outside, an' we stepped out smart to keep ourselves warm. It seemed a long walk to the magazine, but we got there at last, stumblin' along in the snow, with only the corporal's lantern to show us the path.

"The two chaps we relieved was Bill Hatchett an' Happy Johnson, an' they wasn't sorry to see us. I can tell you.

"'Any report?' sez the Corporal.

"'No, Corporal,' sez Happy, an' I thought by the light of the lantern he looked white, 'only me an' Bill heard some funny noises.'

"'Like what?' sez the Corporal,

"'Like a man laughin',' sez Johnson.

"'You've been dreamin',' sez the Corporal, 'quick march.'

"Me an' Nobby watched 'em disappearin' down the hill, the Corporal's lamp a-waggin' till they reached the guard-room.

"'Cheerful blighter,' sez Nobby.

"Nothin' happened for a quarter of an hour. We heard the bells in the town strike quarter-past twelve, an' we marched round the magazine an' pulled up by the sentry box. We was talkin' quietly about fellers we knew, when suddenly Nobby sez—

"'What's that?'

"We listened. Then we heard something far away.

"'It's a bugle.' sez Nobby, in a whisper,

"Sure enough it was. As clear as a bell it came through the snow, an there wasn't any mistake about it.

"'It's the assembly,' sez Nobby.

"The assembly at half-past twelve on Christmas night means something extraordinary. They don't parade the garrison at midnight for nothing.

"'It can't be a fire?' sez Nobby, 'because we'd have heard the fire bugle?'

"He propped his rifle up against the magazine an' put both hands to his mouth an' shouted, 'Guard, turn out.'

"We shouted twice, an' then we heard another sound, a sound that made icy shivers run down our backs. It was somebody laughin' quietly, an' close at hand. I had my rifle at the charge in a second, and Nobby snatched up his.

"'Halt, who comes there?' he shouted.

Nobody answered for a second, then we heard the laugh again.

"'Halt, who comes there?' Nobby shouted again. 'Stand, or I'll fire!'

"I heard the bolt of his rifle snick open an' snap close again. Down below we could see the Corporal's lantern winkin', an' by the way it jerked I could tell he was running.

"'Smithy,' whispers Nobby, there's somebody hidin' round the corner of the magazine—that "assembly" means something—halt!'

"We saw a movement by the wall, A figure crouching, it looked like, an' Nobby raised his rifle an' took aim.

"'Come out of that!' he called, 'or you're a dead man.'

"We waited then a voice said softly—

"'Nobby.'

"Nobby lowered his rifle.

"'Good God,' he whispered, 'it's poor old Jaggers—he's escaped. That's what the assembly was for.'

"'Nobby,' sez the voice again.

"'Yes,' sez Nobby softly.

"'I know my lines, Nobby,' sez the voice

'Behold in me the Demon King,

I'm up to every single thing,'

"The Corporal an' the file of the guard was quite close now.

"'What's wrong?' shouted the Corporal.

"'Show a light, Corporal,' sez Nobby.

"When the light came, Jaggers was lyin' on the ground. He wore his demon king dress an' was perished with cold. Nobby knelt down an' lifted his head, an' Jaggers smiled.

"I took off my overcoat an' tucked it round him.

"'Nobby,' he sez softly, 'do I know my lines?'

"'No one better, old feller,' sez Nobby gently.

"Jaggers shut his eyes.

"'I heard a man say you were at No. 2, so I thought I'd come an' tell you I knew 'em,' he said. ' I'm going to have a sleep now. I'll feel better when I wake up.'

"Poor old Jaggers never did wake up."

## CHAPTER VII

## SMITHY—AMBASSADOR

"There's a lot of fun in the army," said Smithy, "and there's a lot of blooming tragedy, too. In my service I've seen things that'd upset a sentimental cove like you something dreadful. Not the things you see on Christmas almanacs wot the grocer gives away, mind you. Not red soldiers dyin' on green battlefields an' dreamin' of blue mothers; but real, honest tragedies, with no hank whatever.

"I remember a young feller joining the battalion about ten years ago. A nice, quiet, pleasant-spoken feller, who you could tell with half an eye was a tip-topper. He was a clean soldier 'an went about his work without talking, but me an' Nobby noticed something about him that we didn't altogether like. We got two posts a day at that time, and every morning an' night this chap used to waylay the postman an' ask if there was any letter for Private Morris, but none seemed to come.

"He waited an' waited, and it got quite a reg'lar thing to see Morris waiting patiently outside the barrack-room for the postman who brought no letter. One day Morris got up as usual. To our surprise instead of sayin' 'Not to-day,' as be usually did, the postman fished a letter out of his bag an' handed it to Morris, who stuffed it into his pocket an' walked away.

"Nobby an' me was fairly friendly with him, so after a bit we walked down to find Morris. Naturally we thought he was one of those fellers who get a bit of allowance from pa, and Nobby sez, 'The best thing we can do, Smithy, is to go down an' prevent this pore young chap from wastin' the money he's got from home.'

"We found Morris in the back field. He was lying down under a tree, an' his head was on his arm.

"'What cheer, Morris?' sez Nobby, an' was going on to say something about coming into money when we saw Morris' face. I tell you it gave us a turn, for it was as white as death, an' there was something in his eyes that made me shiver.

"I nudged Nobby an' started to walk away, for I could see that Morris was in trouble, but Nobby had seen something, too, and wasn't going to be put off.

"'Hullo, Morris,' he sez, as cheerful as anything, 'somebody left you a fortune?' Morris didn't answer, but dropped his eyes on to the ground, and than I saw Nobby s game.

"He sort of sauntered up casually to where Morris lay, then, stooping quick as lightning, he jerked something from underneath his coat. Nobby was as cool as a blooming ice factory.

"'What's this?' he sez quite surprised. 'I'm blowed if it ain't a revolver, Smithy; where did you get it, Morris?'

"'Give it me!' sez Morris hoarsely.

"'Not me,' sez Nobby very calm. Infantry soldiers ain't supposed to have revolvers—especially infantry soldiers what have had letters from people that makes 'em look like dead men. Morris,' he sez, and Nobby was very earnest—for Nobby, 'is it money or is it a girl because neither of 'em's worth—that.'

"Morris made no answer, but laid face downwards with his head on his arm.

"'Money,' sez Nobby, is hard to get hold of I admit, but girls is fairly plentiful; but gettin' money an' gettin' a girl is child's play compared with getting' a new blooming head once you've started blowing it off with a cheap pistol.'

"Morris groaned a little, an' turned over.

"'Leave me in peace, Clark,' he sez.

"'That's all right,' sez Nobby, cheerful; 'it's leavin' you in pieces wot I'm worryin' about. I ain't going away from here, Morris, till you tell me an' Smithy all about it. And if me an' Smithy think it's bad enough to shoot yourself over, why, we'll go away an' leave you to it—we can't do fairer than that.'

"It was a long time before Morris would chuck his trouble off his chest, but bimeby he up an' made a clean breast of it. It was all about a girl, like Nobby said it would be. Morris didn't like telling us at first, but as soon as he began he told us everything, even to the girl's name and where she lived. It appears that Morris was in love with some girl who was in love with him, and they had a bit of a quarrel, so he had a row and went away and enlisted. From what I could make out the girl had a lot of money of her own, and Morris had about three an' tuppence with prospects—being a rising young feller in the painting line of business. An' her having money and him having none gave him the needle, especially when people said he was after the brass. So the end of it was he went away, leaving a letter, saying her money was between him and her, an' he never wanted to hear from her again, an' if she wrote to him she was to address the letter care of a bank in London. Well, the letter she sent was the one he got that morning. She said in very high-class language that if a chap allowed money to upset his love, he wasn't any chap for her, so farewell, an' never let me hear from you again. N.B.—My address is now 44 Elgin Gardens, S.W.

"Nobby was very indignant when Morris finished tellin' the tale.

"So that's what's makin' you shoot yourself, is it,' he sez, highly disgusted, 'because a girl with a b t of money wants to marry you?'

"'She doesn't want to marry me any more,' sez Morris very miserably.

"'If she's got any sense she don't,' sez Nobby, 'but if she's an ordinary kind of girl she'll want to marry you more than ever.'

"The end of it was that Nobby talked an' talked an' talked till Morris got ashamed of himself an' promised he wouldn't do any more monkey tricks. Me an' Nobby sold the revolver that night in town for eight-and-sixpence, an' had several drinks out of the money. 'What I can't understand,' sez Nobby, 'is what state of mind a feller gets into when he won't marry a girl with a bit of ready. Refuses to marry a girl because she's got money! Why, its blasphemous!'

"We had a long talk over the matter that night, an' next morning me an' Nobby paraded at the orderly room an' asked for special leave of absence to go to London.

"Going up in the train that afternoon we made up what we should say.

"'What's the name again, Smith?' sez Nobby.

"'Miss Dorothy Garratt,' I sez.

"'Very good,' sez Nobby, noddin' his head. 'Now, Smithy, you leave all the talking to me. I'll say to her, "Miss, are you aware that your fiancé is at present a soldier an' breakin' his bloomin' heart? " "Good heavens, no!" she'll say. "It's a fact, miss," I'll say. "He's in the Anchester Regiment, what's just going out to war, an' it's six to four taken an' offered that he'll be killed—"'

"'Him being a reckless chap owin' to being in love,' I sez.

"'What you an' me are, Smithy,' sez Nobby, 'are ambassadors.'

"'What's that?' I sez.

"'A feller that sticks his nose into other people's trouble without bein' asked,' sez Nobby.

"Somehow, the nearer we got to the business the less me an' Nobby liked it. We sat over tea for a long time deciding what time we'd go, and we kept putting it off, an' putting it off.

"It was about nine o'clock before we got to Elgin Gardens. No. 44 was a big, rich-looking house, and we stood outside for quite a long time.

"'I expect they've gone to bed,' sez Nobby ; 'it seems a shame to disturb 'em.'

"'Let's come to-morrow,' I sez; but Nobby sort of drew a long breath an' went up the steps an' knocked. I've always said about Nobby that you don't know what he can't do, an' the genteel way he rat-tatted on that door showed his education.

"We was both making up our minds to walk down the steps an' pretend that we'd knocked at the wrong house, when the door opened and there was a footman with a nice, white shirt-front.

"'We want to see Miss Dorothy Garratt,' sez Nobby as bold as brass.

"Bimeby the footman came back, an' sez the young lady would see us. He led the way upstairs—and the carpet on the stairs was soft an' crunchy, like snow—an' into a big room furnished better than any private bar I've seen.

"'Stand where you are, Smithy,' says Nobby; 'if you move you'll break something.'

"We waited about two minutes, when the door opened an' in came the prettiest girl you ever dreamt about.

"'You wish to see me about something,' she sez inquiringly.

"'Well, it's like this, miss,' sez Nobby, lookin' up at the ceiling, 'me an' Smithy thought we'd like to see you an' have a talk about a certain party. It's nothing to do with us, but he's a comrade of ours, so to speak an' we don't think it right.'

"The young lady looked puzzled.

"'I'm afraid—' she sez.

"'So are we,' sez Nobby quick, 'that's just what we are, we're afraid too. We're a respectable regiment, an' we don't want no horrible tragedies. What we want is a quiet, peaceful life, an' no bloomin' upsets— begging your pardon—an' the sooner you make him leave the regiment the better.'

"The girl looked more puzzled than ever.

"'I really don't know what you are talking about,' she sez.

"'Well,' sez Nobby, 'to put it plain an' above board, the chap's name is Morris.'

"'Morris,' she sez slowly. 'I'm afraid I don't know anybody of that name.'

"My heart went down into my boots, and so did Nobby's. I could see that by his dial. Poor old Nobby looked like a chap that's been dreamin' he's on furlough an' wakes up to find hisself in clink.

"'I'm afraid, miss,' he sez sorrowfully, 'we've made a slight error. We thought we was doin' a chap a good turn, but we've come to the wrong address. I'll bid you good evening, miss.'

"'Wait a moment,' she sez quick. Tell me about this Morris.'

"Nobby shook his head.

"'It's no good tellin' you, miss,' he sez, 'it would only make you feel miserable. He's a young chap of ours, who's only lately joined the army, an' he's in love with a girl, in consequence of which he was going to shoot hisself, only me an' Smithy stopped him.'

"'What is he like?' she sez, an' I could see her face had gone suddenly white. 'Is he tall?

"'Fairly,' see Nobby.

"'With blue eyes?' she sez quick.

"'I couldn't tell you about his eyes,' sez Nobby, but he's got a scar on one side of his head.'

"'Yes, yes,' she sez eager.

"'And he's a painter chap,' I sez.

"'A painter?' she gasps. 'Why, it's Jack, and he's enlisted, and he was going to shoot himself, and—'

"There was a lot more stuff like that. She asked about fifty questions in about ten seconds, an' she rung the bell an' ordered dinner for us.

"She was in a terrible state of mind, although Nobby told her it was no good thinkin' about going to Anchester that night.

"'Whatever you do, miss.' sez Nobby, 'don't you tell Morris to-morrow that me an' Smithy have seen you. Just write to him to meet you. There's a nice quiet hotel with a big garden where you can see him.'

"'How can I thank you, Mr Clark?' she sez, with tears in her eyes.

"'Don't mention It, miss,' sez Nobby, very agitated.

"She walked over to a desk, opened a drawer, an' took something out.

"'You must let me pay your expenses to London, she sez, an' she held out two banknotes to Nobby.'

"'Thank you, miss,' sez Nobby quietly, 'but our expenses ain't worth mentionin'. We're very much obliged, but we couldn't think of takin' money.'

"'I'm sorry,' she sez, flushing. 'I'm afraid I've hurt your feelings. Is there nothing I can do for you to show my gratitude?'

"Nobby shook his head.

"'Nothin', miss,' he sez. ' I've only one inclination just now—and so has Smithy.'

"'What is yours?' she sez.

"'A pint of Burton, thank you, miss,' sez Nobby.

"'Mine's the same,' I sez."

## CHAPTER VIII

### HOGMANAY

"Nobby Clark was tellin' me a yarn the other day," said Private Smith, "about two blokes who got blown up in a quarry. One called Jack an' the other Bill. They used to hate the sight of each other, but they was put in beds next to one another, an' as Jack lost his nose an' Bill lost his ear in the explosion, they couldn't very well pass any unpleasant remarks between theirselves. Jack wasn't a bad-feelin' sort of chap, so on New Year's Day he ups an' sez—

"'An happy New Ye'r to you, Bill.'

"The other bloke got very wild.

"'An' a happy new nose to you,' he snarls, 'don't be so bloomin' personal.'

"What made Nobby tell me this was the nice kind sentiments that are goin' cheap just about now, where lots of fellers go round wishin' people they don't know, things they don't mean.

"Spud Murphy is one of the chaps who always gets sloppy about this time of the year, an' when he came up to Nobby a few days ago an' sez, 'A happy New Year', Nobby turns round an' sez, 'I don't want your good wishes. I've told you so about six years runnin', an' if I have to tell you again you'll get a dig in the eye!'

"New Year's Day," continued Smithy, "ain't nothing in the Army unless you've got some pals in an Highland regiment. The 'Jocks' celebrate New Year's Day just the same as camels celebrate any day they happen to strike a river—they take in enough supplies to last 'em the rest of the year.

"There was a 'Jock' by the name of Ogilvie when we was quartered next to the 91st, who was a rare friend of mine an' Nobby's.

"He was one of them Scotsmen you never read about, freehanded an' liberal, an' he came from a little village called Glasgow—which is why he was called a Highlander.

"One Year's Eve he sez to me an' Nobby—

"'Come into our barracks for hogmanay.'

"'No thanks,' sez Nobby, 'I'm Church of England.'

"So Ogilvie explained it was nothin' to do with religion.

"'Is it something to drink?' sez Nobby, an' Ogilvie sez yes, so me an' Nobby said we'd be there.

"We turned up all right, and there was everything of the best, an' chaps was singin' an' chaps was dancin', an' one chap was playin' the bagpipes something awful.

"'I don't know why you call it hogmanay,' sez Nobby; 'it tastes like whisky—perhaps it's the Scotch way of spellin' it.'

"'It is,' sez Ogilvie.

"As I was for guard the next day I took a lot of water with my hogmanay, an' went away early. As I left, I heard Nobby tellin' a 'Jock'—

"'I'm a genuine Scotchman myself—having been born in Scotland—my father always wore kilts. an' me sister married a chap in the butterscotch line—'

"I didn't hear the rest of it. Nobby is what you might call 'adaptable.' Nobby got back to barracks about 3 a.m. I heard him, an' so did everybody else. He was singin' a song about a girl who was 'bonnie' an' lived in a 'bonnie' house in 'bonnie' Scotland, an' the way he'd got hold of the Scotch accent was simply marvellous.

"He was singin' another song about 'bonnie Highland Mary,' when the corporal of the room sez—

"'Now then, Mr. Blooming Clark, not so much "bonnie"; get to bed, or I'll be puttin' you where the pigs won't bite you.'

"Nobby must have got a lot of hogmanay into him, for he ups and sez—

"'Hoot, mon—dinna blether.'

"'What's he say?' sez the corporal.

"'Ye'll tak' the high road, an' I'll tak' the low,' sings Nobby.

"'Ye'll tak' the road to the guard-room,' sez the corporal, getting out of bed an' scrambling into his clothes, an' he orders me an' another chap to get out of bed an' escort Nobby to the clink.

"'What!' sez Nobby, lookin' reproachfully at me—'what! ma wee freen', ma brither Scot, ma bonnie Smithy—'

"'Shut up!' I sez, an' we led him over to the guardroom. He didn't say much, except that it was a 'braw munelicht nicht the nicht,' an' what that meant I don't know.

"The guard took his boots off an' put him in a cell, an', after he'd called the sergeant of the guard a 'low Southerner' or somethin' equally insultin', be went to sleep.

"When I took his breakfast across next mornin' he looked a bit silly.

"'Let this be a warnin' to you, Smithy,' he sez very solemn, 'don't take foreign drinks—beer's all right an' whisky's all right—but hogmanay is poison.'

"Now, everybody likes Nobby, an' the corporal of the room didn't want to jug him for drunk,' so he made it up with the sergeant of the guard that Nobby was to be 'crimed' for creatin' a disturbance in barracks after lights-out, and Nobby accepted the three days' C.B. with a thankful heart.

"The next day he said he was goin' to join the A.T.A. (Army Temperance Association), an' asked me if I'd join, too, so I said I would, an' we become members—section 'B' members, drink as much as you can carry, but don't make a beast of yourself—that's section B.'

(In justice to that admirable institution, I must explain that the membership is divided into two sections, A being for total abstainers, B for the moderate drinkers.)

"Our Sergeant-Major's cracked on drink," continued Smithy, "he can't see a bit of grease on a belt without thinkin' it's alco-what-is-it? Lots of chaps joined the A.T.A. to get a lance-stripe; me an' Nobby joined to start the New Year well.

"'Glad to see you, Private Smith; glad to see you, Private Clark,' sez the S.-M., shakin. hands with me an' Nobby as if we was human bein's.

"'Are you goin' to join?'

"'Thank you kindly, sir,' sez Nobby. ' I don't mind if I do.'

"'Shall it be section "A"?' sez the Sergeant-Major, smilin'.'

"'Make it "B," sir,' sez Nobby, 'an' we'll try to work back to "A" gradual.'

"So we puts our names down, an' after singin' a bit, an' hearin' two recruits recite 'Billy's Rose' an' 'The Last Shot,' we goes out.

"Just as we got up near the canteen, we heard some one say—

"'Here comes the new bun-thumpers; let's tempt 'em,' an' out comes Spud Murphy with harf a gallon.

"'What! me true blues!' sez Spud, offerin' the can, 'passin' by your old haunts without droppin' in? Take a swig, Nobby.'

"So Nobby took the harf gallon an' looked at it, serious.

"Then he sez, 'Away, tempter,' but held on to the beer.

"All the chaps the beer belonged to was larfin' like anything, an' saying, 'Go on, Nobby, break out—a little drop won't hurt you.'

But Nobby shook his 'ead, sorrerful.

"'I ain't got the face to,' he sez sadly, 'after me takin' the pledge an' all,' but he lifted the beer all the same, an' took a long sip. Then he handed the can to me an' whispers, 'Drink hearty, Smithy,' which I did.

"Then we handed the can back.

"Spud looks inside, and then looks at us.

"'You've drunk it all,' he sez, very fierce.

"'I know I have, Spud,' sez Nobby sorrerfully; 'I know I have—don't tempt me to drink any more.'

"'Don't worry yourself about that,' sez Spud hotly; what about the bloomin' pledge you've signed?'

"'That,' sez Nobby slowly, 'is what you might call a temp'ry pledge—and only applies to hogmanay. I'm goin' to keep off hogmanay for twelve months at least.'"


CHAPTER IX

ON FINANCE

Private Smith was in a philosophical frame of mind.

"The world's a funny little place," he said sententiously. "As Nobby Clark was sayin' the other day. dear friends, wot you'd lost sight of and hoped was dead, are always croppin' up an' sayin', 'Hullo. Nobby, what about that two bob you borrowed in Bombay?'

"Nobby sez he read a sayin' about good people dying young, and that's true. Fellers you owe money to never die. If you read a bit in the paper about a feller runnin' to catch a train an' droppin' dead, or about a gentleman fallin' from the fourth floor when he's cleanin' the bedroom winders, you can bet nobody owes money to him.

"Antony Gerrard, esquire—him I told you about—sez, 'I neither borrow nor lend,' when Nobby tried to touch him the other day, so Nobby sez—

"'I don't want Scripture, Tony, I want a bob.'

"'If you take my advice—' says Antony.

"'I don't want advice, I want a bob till pay day,' sez Nobby, very patient.

"'Him that goes borrowin' goes sorrowin',' sez Antony.

"'I don't want advice, and I don't want poetry,' sez Nobby, still very patient, 'I want one blooming shillin' or twelve blooming pence.'

"'The end of it was that Antony parted with eleven-pence an' two half-penny stamps.

"I know lots of people who spend money to make the time pass. But there ain't any quicker way than borrowin' a couple of bob till Wednesday. Why, you ain't got time to put the money in your pocket before Wednesday's come an' gorn!

"Nobby's the best borrower I know. Sometimes he pays back and sometimes he don't. He's very careless in money affairs, is Nobby; and when you see him cutting bits out of the paper about people who've suddenly lost their memory, you can be pretty sure that he owes a bit, an' is sort of making up an alibi.

"He owed a feller named Boysey—a red-headed chap —close on ten bob for months an' months.

"When Boysey came up to him on pay day to collect, Nobby's face got a worried look.

""What about that ten bob?' sez Boysey.

"'What's my name?' sez Nobby, very bewildered.

"That staggered Boysey.

"'Why, Nobby Clark,' he sez.

"'Ha, ha!' sez Nobby faintly. 'Ha, ha! What a funny name!'

"Boysey got scared, and walked away quick, pretendin' he was in a hurry to get to the canteen before it shut.

"I met him comin' across the square, and he looked upset.

"'Pore old Nobby's gorn off his chump,' he sez excitedly, 'gorn clean off his bloomin' napper.'

"'What's up?' I sez.

"'Why, he don't know his own name,' sez Boysey, all of a tremble, 'and he's laughin' and ravin' like a lunatic.'

"When I got up to the room I found Nobby sitting on a bed trying to make up a limerick.

"'Hullo, balmy!' I sez.

"'Hullo, Smithy,' be sez. 'Where's Boysey?'

"'Gorn to get the key of the padded cell,' I sez. 'You're a nice feller, losing your memory.'

"'Smithy,' he sez, very earnest, 'it's the only thing I've got that's worth losing.'

"I've never discovered what Nobby does with his money. I asked him once, an' he told me he was supporting a widdered mother. Then I got to find out that he hadn't got a mother, and I told him so.

"Nobby wasn't a bit upset at being found out.

"'When I said "mother,"' he sez calmly, 'I meant my Uncle Bill, who's been a widdered mother to me.'

"The company officer asked him once—

"'What do you do with your money, Clark—I'm always hearing from people you owe money to?'

"'I'm savin' up, sir,' he sez.

"'But why don't you pay your debts?' sez the officer.

"'Nobby was very wild about this afterwards.

"'How can a chap save up if he's got to pay his debts?' he sez to me. 'Payin' your debts Is simply wastin' your money—why it's worse than drink!'

"From what Nobby said, it appeared he was saving up to go into business. Last Wednesday week the fellers were chaffin' Nobby about this.

"Nobby took no offence.

"'I'm going,' sez he, 'to open a high-class money-lender's.'

"We was so took back that none of us could speak.

"'A high-class what?' sez Spud.

"'Money-lender's,' sez Nobby, quite calm; 'people are getting so stingy in barracks that you can't borrow a bob when you want it without 'em coming to get it back again. So I'm going to lend money on a new plan. If you can't pay it back, go on owing it.

"The funny thing about Nobby's plan was that it was so simple. All that you had to do If you wanted money was to go and ask for it. It was so blooming simple that a good number of chaps who wanted money pretty badly, got suspicious.

"Boysey called a meetin' of Nobby's creditors.

"'It's like this,' sez Boysey. Nobby owes me ten bob, and he owes Pug Wilson four bob, and Antony two bob, and if he's got any money to lend, the first thing that he ought to do is to pay back the like of us. I vote that we all go to Nobby, one at a time, and borrow what we can, and when we've got the money stick to it.'

"All Nobby's creditors said that it was a good plan, and they tossed up odd man out to see who'd go first.

"Boysey won it, so up he went to Nobby.

"'Nobby,' sez he, ' I'd be greatly obliged if you'd lend me five bob.'

"'Certainly,' sez Nobby, pullin' out a bit of paper and a pencil.

"'What's this?' sez Boysey.

"'That's a paper what you've got to sign.' sez Nobby.

"'Whaffor?' sez Boysey, very indignant. 'I didn't ask you to sign an I.O.U. when I lent you ten bob.'

"'This is different,' sez Nobby, very serious, 'this ain't an I.O.U. it's a U.O.Me.'

"When Boysey signed his name Nobby collected a bob from him.

"'I've got to make a lot of inquiries,' sez Nobby, 'before I lend money.'

"Boysey didn't like parting, but he thought it was worth while.

"Spud Murphy wanted to borrow two shillin's till pay day, and when Nobby tried to corral a tanner for inquiries Spud sez Nobby was a swindler.

"But all this time Nobby was lendin' money to other fellers right enough. Fourpence for tuppence, an' sixpence for fourpence, an' it looked as though he'd got a good thing on. When fellers came who Nobby didn't trust he used to pull out his bit of paper an' make 'em sign, then get a shillin' out of 'em for inquiries.

"One day Nobby sez to me—

"'I'm doin' so well that I'm gettin' frightened. I made four an' tuppence last week profit. Everybody's paid back, an' nobody owes anything.'

"I think Nobby must have lost his head just about then, because he lent money to everybody.

"He came to me about a week after, lookin' 'orribly wild, an' the way be went on gnashing his teeth an' saying he'd kill old Boysey was as good as a play. Boysey hadn't paid back the five, and, what was worse, he'd put all the other fellers up to a wrinkle or two.

"'I'll show 'em,' sez Nobby, and that night him an' me went over to the canteen together to collect accounts.

"The first feller we saw was Spud Murphy.

"'Hullo, Spud,' sez Nobby, tryin' to be cheerful.

"'Where am I?' sez Spud.

"'You're in the canteen drinkin' another man's beer,' sez Nobby.

"'Who am I?' sez Spud, in a far-away voice.

"'Look here,' sez Nobby, very wrathy, 'don't you come them lost memory games on me, because I invented 'em—see? If you want to know who you are, I can tell you in twice. You're a bottle-nosed Houndsditch Irishman wot owes me two bob.'

"'I feel strange,' sez Spud in a wild way.

"'You'll feel stranger,' sez Nobby, chuckin' his cap on the ground 'you'll feel so strange that your mother won't know her darling child if you don't fork out that three bob.'

"'Two bob,' sez Spud, comin' round quick.

"'Three bob,' sez Nobby; 'two bob I lent you and a bob extra for the trouble in getting it back.'

"It was worth all the extra bobs Nobby could get, because all the chaps who owed money to Nobby got a fit or something as soon as Nobby got near him. Pug Wilson's memory was worse than Spud's, only Pug's way was more aggravatin' than Spud's.

"'What about that two bob you owe me?' sez Nobby, very pleasant.

"'What two bob?' sez Pug.

"'The two bob I lent you one night,' sez Nobby.

"'Was it rainin'?' sez Pug, looking very puzzled.

"'I didn't notice the weather,' sez Nobby, getting warm; 'I only noticed that I lent you two bob—two separate shillin's.'

"Pug was more puzzled than ever.

"'Did one have a hole in it?' he sez.

"'I didn't notice the hole,' sez Nobby shortly, 'I only noticed—'

"'Where was I?' sez Pug.

"'Here,' sez Nobby.

"'Was my back to the counter, or was I sitting down?' sez Pug, still puzzled.

"Nobby sort of drew a long breath.

"'Pug,' he sez kindly, 'if you ask me any more questions I'll put you down and tread on you. Pug, your life's worth two bob—pass it over.'

"By the time Nobby had collected twelve shillin's he was getting grey, and when Boysey came into the canteen I saw something was goin to happen. Nobby didn't see him come in, so I slipped over to Boysey.

"'Boysey,' I sez, quick, 'you owe five bob to Nobby. When he asks for it don't do the funny business or the lorst memory business—I'm advisin' you as a friend.'

"Just then Nobby saw him, and braced himself up; then he came over. Boysey didn't make his face blank or have a fit or anything. He waited till Nobby came up.

"'Five shillin's,' sez Nobby, very short, 'and look lively.'

"'Will you have it now,' sez Boysey, as bold as brass, 'or will you wait till quarter-day?'

"'I'll have it,' sez Nobby, chokin', 'whilst you're alive, Boysey. Don't worry me. Boysey, there's madness in me family. I've got a brother who killed a policeman an' another one who backs Captain Joe's naps....'

"'That night Nobby said to me—

"'Smithy, let this be a warnin' to you. Never get hold of any money an' never lend it. The happiest feller is the feller that borrows. He's got nothin' to worry him—it's the feller that lends that's got all the worryin' to do—let's go down town and blue this cursed wealth.'"

## CHAPTER X

## THE HEROES

"Being a hero is not much catch nowadays," said Private Smith, gloomily.

"Not that I've ever gone in for that line of business except once. I've always thought it was bad for the eyesight. We had a feller in ours once who stopped a runaway cab in the High Street, and the Mayor and Corporation gave him a gold watch and chain. It quite altered the young feller. Before, he was the sort of chap who wasn't above coming back to barracks an hour or so after lights-out, as genial, kind-hearted and let's-have-another sort of man as you could wish to meet. But as soon as he got into the Hero class, he was changed. It was perfectly sickenin' to watch him. He'd start at half-past seven by pulling out his bright gold watch.

"'Hullo!' he says; 'I've got another two hours yet.' It was one of them watches with a hole in the case for you to see the time by. There wasn't any necessity to open it, but old Wilkie—that was his name—used to open the case every time and hold the watch close up to his eyes. Sometimes he wasn't sure it was going: then he used to hold it up to his ear for about three minutes, with all the chaps in the bar not daring to breathe while he heard if the 'tick-tick' was all right.

"Being a hero makes you short-sighted and hard of hearing, especially if you get a cheap rolled-gold American clock for being one. And every hour, regular, all through the evening, out would come his watch to see if it was time to get back to barracks.

"That's what fed me and Nobby up with the hero trade, and when the war started and heroes began to get as common as V.C.'s in a Highland regiment, we thought it was about time for Wilkie to forget all about the cab-horse performance.

"It was when the regiment was on the train going up to the front that Nobby told Wilkie what he thought.

"'Wilkie,' he sez, 'put away that cheap little ticker of yours and pay a little attention to your Uncle Nobby. Wilkie, the hero market is overcrowded. You're amongst the fourth-class shots in the hero squad, Wilkie. In a week or so this blooming battalion will be so full up with heroes that you won't be able to walk a yard without treading on one. And they'll be real heroes, Wilkie, with their pictures in the papers, and if you start giving yourself airs about stopping that poor old cab-horse, wot wouldn't 'urt a fly, you'll be in much about the same position as a selling-plater in the Jockey Club Stakes.'

And sure enough what Nobby said came true. There was Hero Jordan, who brought up the ammunition wagon at Nelspruit; and Hero White, who carried 'Kinky' James out of the line of fire when he was wounded; and Hero Tarbut, the chap who saved the pom-pom—in fact the heroes in the regiment multiplied like rabbits.

"When the regiment got home again after the war we was all heroes. People we didn't know used to stop us in the street and shake hands with us, and uncles of mine I'd never heard of in my life sent me invitations to spend a week with 'em.

"You couldn't walk a yard without something being in the newspapers about it:—

'We hear that Mr. George Smith, our respected fellow-townsman, is entertaining his nephew, Private Smith, of the Anchester Regiment, who heroically fought at Ladysmith.'

"That was years and years ago, and the last time I went down to see Uncle George I got into the paper again:—

Isn't it time that the military authorities took steps to save Mudbury from the plague of soldiers? They seem to swarm in our streets, and our respected fellow-townsman, Mr. George Smith, has had an unpleasant experience. A drunken private, claiming to be Mr. Smith's nephew, called at his house and was very properly refused admittance. Whereupon he struck Mr. Smith in the chest and made off.'

"The hero business is played out now. The heroes are carrying coal and drinking beer like ordinary people, and as to old Wilkie—why, even he ain't one—and he was a civilian hero, too.

"I was speaking to Wilkie the other day about it.

"'I give up bein' a hero when the gold began to wear off the watch and leave little black patches,' sez Wilkie sadly.

"'What we want,' sez Nobby Clark, 'is a heroes' trade union.'

"'At so much a week?' says Spud Murphy unpleasantly, but Nobby took no notice.

"'We want all the heroes to join together and stick up for their rights,' he sez—Nobby was very great on societies and things of that sort. Well, the fellers were rather struck with the idea, but they was a bit suspicious of Nobby. But Nobby took his solemn oath, see-that-wet-see-that-dry-cut-my-throat-if-I-tell-a-lie, that he wasn't going to make a penny out of it, and it was agreed that a society should be formed for the Encouragement of Heroes.

"We had a meeting next night, and Nobby took the chair.

"'The first business is to get the heroes,' sez Nobby; 'now who's the first?'

"Nobody answered for a bit, but Wilkie coughed and looked round the room to show the fellows he was there.

"'Well,' sez Nobby, after a bit. ' I'll put myself down first.'

"'Wot have you done in the hero line?' demanded Spud loudly.

"Nobby eyed his steadily.

"'Friends and comrades all,' sez Nobby, shutting his eyes, like he always does when he makes a speech, 'I don't want to boast, but once on the line of march, when the regiment was on 'arf rations, I gave Pug Wilson my rations because he was hungry. Ain't that true, Smithy?'

"'It is so,' I sez, but it was because Nobby is what I call a dainty feeder an' very particular as to what he eats.

"So Nobby puts his name down.

"I next propose Smithy,' he sez, owing to his heroic conduct at Bloemfontein.'

"All the fellers were puzzling their heads trying to think what I'd done special at Bloemfontein, and I was a bit puzzled myself'.

"'When was that, Nobby?' I sez.

"'The night we pinched the chickens,' he sez calmly.

"'Here, hold hard,' sez Spud; 'there's nothing heroic about stealin' chickens.'

"'That,' sez Nobby, as calm as you please, 'depends on the chicken. These chickens were the fiercest chickens you ever saw.' So he put my name down.

"A lot of fellers had come to the meeting not hoping to get into the Heroes' Society, but when they saw how easy it was, and that there was nothing to pay, they started to hand in their names.

"Hoppy Sands joined because he once helped a policeman to take a drunken man to the station; Harry Gill came in because he was once bit by a dog.

"'I'll come in, Nobby,' sez Spud, who'd been hanging back a bit.

"'What have you ever done besides time?' sez Nobby.

"'Never mind what I've done,' sez Spud loudly; 'but if I'm not more of a hero than some of you fellers I'll eat my boots.'

"Nobby and Spud ain't very good friends, and Nobby got up and walked over to Spud.

"'Do I understand,' he sez, 'that you consider yourself a better hero than me?'

"'I do,' sez Spud.

"'For why?' sez Nobby quietly.

"'Because I could jolly well knock your fat head orf,' sez Spud, as fierce as anything.

"'The meeting is adjourned,' sez Spud, whilst me and this other hero go outside and see who is the best hero of the two.'

"It came out in the end that Nobby was a black eye and a tooth better hero than Spud, and it led to a lot of unpleasantness afterwards. What's more it ki-boshed the society, because Spud found out that all the encouragement he got was from a lot of chaps who stood round and said, 'Go on, Nobby; give him the upper cut. Smash him, Nobby; oh, well hit, sir!' and things like that.

"Spud said that the Society for Encouraging Heroes only encouraged Nobby, and it was a bit too one-sided.

"The row went on for a couple of months. One night Nobby was coming back to barracks a little after twelve. He'd been over to see a gentleman who owns a rat-pit at Stokely, and he had missed his train and had to walk. He was taking a short-cut across some fields, and had just reached the big house that stands at the end of the town, a mile from the nearest house, when he heard an awful row. A girl came shrieking down the drive. Nobby could see she had her nightdress on and knew there was trouble.

"She was sobbing and shrieking, and Nobby caught her arm.

"'Here,' sez Nobby shaking her, 'what's the matter? What's biting ye?'

"He couldn't get anything out of her for a minute, and then a light through the trees told him what was the matter.

"'Fire!' shouts Nobby, and shook the girl.

"'Is there anybody in the house,' he roars, but the girl was nearly mad with fright.

"Nobby sez he gave her a smack on the head to pull her together.

"'Two children,' she wails, and clung on to Nobby. From what he could gather the master and misses were out at a ball and the other servants were away too. She babbled something about a 'soldier,' but Nobby didn't wait to hear. He was running up to the house. The front door was open, and the two top floors were ablaze, the flames coming out through the window.

"He took off his belt and ran into the house.

"The hall was full of smoke, but he stumbled along till he found the stairs, and went blundering up with his eyes shut. He got to the first floor, and could hear the fire roaring above. Up to the next flight Nobby ran knocking over the vases and things that the hall was decorated with.

"He didn't know where the kids were, but he guessed it was on the top floor, because being the most dangerous place for children, that's where all nurseries are.

"In the darkness he stumbled into a bath-room, and that was Nobby's salvation, for he had a minute to soak his tunic in water before be started to crawl up the next flight.

"He shouted at the top of his voice—

"'Is anybody there?'

"The smoke and the heat didn't upset Nobby so much as hearing a voice say, 'Yes,' for it was a voice Nobby knew.

"'Hullo, Spud,' he sez in astonishment, and then remembering he wasn't on good terms with him, 'Hullo, hero,' he sez.

"Spud's voice was choked with smoke.

"'Help get these kids downstairs,' he sez, 'you tuppenny-ha'penny chicken thief.'

"Nobby had a reply on the top of his tongue, but the smoke got into his throat, so he groped about for one of the children.

"He found one little curly head, and lifted the child

"'Come on, Spud,' he sez, but he made no answer.

"'Spud!' called Nobby.

"He heard Spud's voice.

"'I'm done,' he sez weakly, 'get the kids out.'

"Nobby found the other child, and went floundering downstairs with the two. He got outside, and laid the children on the grass. He heard people running, and knew that the fire had been discovered; then turned back into the house again. It was harder this time to get upstairs, but he managed it. The top floor was like an oven; the smoke was worse than ever. He shut his eyes tight and went feeling about the landing. By and by he found Spud, who had fallen into a corner.

"'Spud!' he yells, but Spud didn't answer. He was too heavy to carry, but Nobby dragged him to the edge of the stairs and pushed him over, and Spud fell with a crash to the next landing.

"It woke Spud up, but before Nobby could get any sense into him he was unconscious again, so Nobby repeated the performance.

"Just then the firemen came in and got them both out.

"Neither Spud nor Nobby was any the worse for the experience the next morning when they paraded at the orderly room.

"Spud said he felt sore but Nobby said nothing.

"Talk about heroes! The paper was full of it. The Colonel had Nobby and Spud up before him.

"'I am very proud of you men,' sez the Colonel. 'I only regret that the regulations don't allow me to reward you,' he sez.

"'I've had my reward,' sez Nobby; 'I'd go through it all over again for the pleasure of chucking Spud Murphy downstairs!'"

CHAPTER XI

THE COMPETITORS

I

Not the least pleasant characteristic of Smithy is his touching confidence in my omnipotence.

Whenever he sees an article or story of mine in a paper or magazine, you may be sure that he addresses me as the "editor" of that particular production. Should by any chance a play or sketch with which I am remotely connected be in course of performance anywhere near Anchester, I know I shall receive peremptory demands for tickets, on the assumption that I own the theatre.

When Smithy called in at Kensington a few weeks ago and talked vaguely about journalism and the ethics thereof, and made rambling and inconclusive references to the probity of the Press, I asked him to come to the point, and, with an apologetic preamble, he came.

"I don't want you to give yourself away," began Smithy, alarmingly. "You've got to make your livin' as well as anybody else, an' it ain't for me to go pryin' into your business. But Spud Murphy said it's a swindle, an' Nobby said it ain't, an' lots of chaps take one side or the other, so I thought I'd come an' see you—you're the editor of Ideas, ain't you?

I destroyed Smithy's illusion with a word, and his face fell.

"I thought you was," he said reproachfully.

"Well, anyway, you'll know what I want to find out: are limericks swindles?"

I assured him that so far from that, limerick competitions were remarkably fair, and that the efforts of competitors received extraordinary careful scrutiny, and that the best lines won.

"But do the people get it, or does some pal of the editor's get it?" asked Smithy, with brutal directness.

"Why, you owl," I replied, "don't you realise that there are hundreds of disappointed people on the lookout for signs of favouritism, and that every winner's name and address is carefully verified and their family history inquired into by people who have got the same idea as you, and that—"

"That's all right," said Smithy easily; "that's what I say, an' Nobby Clark sez, but we thought we'd inquire first, because a tanner's a lot of money to chuck away.

He fished out from his pocket a paper, which he carefully unfolded, disclosing a newspaper coupon, which, borrowing the terminology of the second-hand bookseller, was " slightly soiled," and this, without preliminary and with due solemnity, he read—

There was an old man of Torbay

Who never had been to a play,

So to Faust he was led,

When he'd seen it he said,

"Well?" said Smithy inquiringly, and I realised he wanted me to suggest a line.

"Work in something about 'the devil to pay,' " I suggested....

Smithy told me the sequel last Wednesday.

"Nobby liked your line, the bit about the devil; so we got a line up, him an' me, an' sent it in.

"All that week we talked about that tanner. Nobby remembered about two hundred ways we might have spent it. Then when the week came round for the prize to be announced Nobby said we ought to forget all about it, an' then it 'ud come as a surprise. So we started tryin' to forget, an' the more we tried, the more we remembered.

"I kept quiet about it for two days, but I was thinkin' all the time what we would do if we got a fiver an' though Nobby said nothin' I could tell it was on his mind.

"On the second day he up, an' spoke.

"'Look here, Smithy,' he sez, 'it's no good of us reckonin' on that limerick; we'll suppose we've lost.'

"'Yes,' I sez.

"'Well, it's all over then,' sez Nobby, pretendin', 'an' we ain't got a prize or nothin'.'

"'That's right,' I sez, pretendin', too.

"'Limericks is swindles,' sez Nobby, very loud.

"'Daylight robbers,' I sez.

"'No more limericks for me,' sez Nobby. 'I've lost once—never again.'

"It got all over barracks that we'd lost, an' fellers who was waitin' to see if we won before they speculated themselves kept their money in their pocket an' said they knew limericks was swindles all along.

"That night, when me an' Nobby was in the canteen, the postman poked his head in the door an' shouts, 'Clark!'

"When Nobby went over to him he hands him a letter, an' Nobby looks at it an' turns pale.

"I looks at it, an' I went cold all over, for on the back flap of the envelope was printed the name of the paper, I looks at Nobby, an' he looks at me.

"'Let's feel that letter, Smithy.' So I gave it him

"'It don't feel very thick,' he sez, p'raps it's a consolation prize.'

"'Let's go up to the barrack-room,' sez Nobby. So up we went an' had a good look at the envelope. There It was right enough—

Private Clark,

B. Company,

1st Anchester Regiment.

"'Shall we open it?' I sez.

"'No,' sez Nobby, 'not yet; get your belt on, an' we'll go down town.'

"So we went out, an' walked down the High Street very solemn, Nobby with the letter in his inside pocket.

"We was walkin' along quite quickly, when suddenly Nobby grabbed me by the arm an' pointed. Over the road was Ruggle's paper shop, an outside was the placard of the limerick paper, and on it was—

OUR LIMERICK
ANCHESTER SOLDIER
WINS £125 4s

"I managed to drag Nobby into the Phoenix Arms.

"'My pal's had a bit of a shock,' I sez to the young lady behind the bar. 'Give me two penn'orth of brandy, miss.'

"'Beer,' sez Nobby, openin' his eyes for a second.

"I got him round after repeating the dose.

"'It's not us,' he sez, sad; 'it ain't thick enough, an' besides, it ain't registered, an' besides, it ain't us.'

"'Let's open it,' I sez, tremblin'.

"'You open it,' sez Nobby.

"'No, you,' I sez.

"Nobby took his penknife an' opened it careful.

"'I'll bet it ain't us,' he sez.

"'I'll bet it ain't us.' I sez.

"He opened the paper. There was a cheque, an' he read it. Then he sez in a far-away voice—

"'Kick me, Smithy—where it hurts,' he sez.

"So I kicked him.

"'Now stick that knife in me,' he sez, ' not too far, but just enough to make me jump.'

"So I did—an' he did jump.

"'Miss,' sez Nobby to the young lady, in his dreamy voice, 'would you be to kind as to tell me what I look like?'

"So she told him, an' that sort of woke Nobby up

"'Thank you,' he sez gruffly; then, 'Smithy, its us!'

"An' it was!

"'Here, Miss,' sez Nobby, excited, 'will you ask the gaffer to step this way?' and the landlord, who's a gentleman, though stout, comes along.

"'What's this?' sez Nobby, holdin' out the cheque. He kept hold of it tight, too.

"'This,' sez the bung, 'why, this is a cheque for £125 4s.' he sez.

"'Can you change it?' sez Nobby.

"The landlord looks at Nobby very suspicious.

"'No,' he sez, very short.

."'Will you give me a hundred quid for it?' sez Nobby. You can keep the rest.'

"'No,' sez the landlord again, an' then calls his potman an' whispers somethin' in his ear.

"'You needn't send for the police,' sez Nobby; it's a limerick wot me an' my pal Smithy's won,' he sez.

"We got out into the street.

"'Let's walk about all night,' sez Nobby, an' make up what well do.' Nobby hadn't had a furlough, no more had I, so next mornin' we paraded before the adjutant.

"When the adjutant sees me an' Nobby he sez—

"'Hello, you're the two fellers that won the limerick prize, aren't you?'

"'Yes,' sez me an' Nobby.

"'Well, what are you gain' to do with the money?' sez the adjutant.

"'Spend it,' sez Nobby.

"'Don't you think you'd better save it for a rainy day?' sez the adjutant.

"'No, sir!' sez Nobby, very firm. 'Smithy an' me are goin' up to London on urgent privit business,' he sez.

"'Were goin' to do it in—in a manner of speakin',' he sez.

"The adjutant looked a bit grave.

"'That's darn' foolish,' he sez.

"'Well, it's like this, sir,' sez Nobby, 'if we stay, in barracks we'll spend it anyway, an' get ourselves into trouble—to say nothin' of gettin' other chaps into trouble,' he sez, very earnest. 'So me an' Private Smith are goin' to London to see what it feels like bein' a millionaire—we shall never have another chance.'

"The adjutant shook his head, but he gave us seven days' leave.

"We got an empty carriage to ourselves, an' Nobby pulled out the money.

"'There's sixty-two for you, an' sixty-two for me,' he sez, ' an' we'd better put the return halves of our tickets in our boots for safety—for we ain't likely to bring back much more than them!'"

## II

"It's a wonderful thing," said Smithy, "how coming into money effec's some people. An uncle of mine lost his memory over a matter of two hundred pound. Couldn't remember people who'd done him kindnesses when he was hard up; couldn't remember money he'd borrowed orf my father an' couldn't pay back; couldn't call to mind hundreds of knowin' people who called on him to wish him luck. Another chap, whose gran'-mother left him a row of houses out Walworth way, used to be a Socialist. Always wore a red tie, an' used hair-oil. Used to carry a banner in a percession, 'Death to the capitalists,' 'We demand more money an' less work,' and 'We demand the right to live.'

"Soon after he come into his houses, a pal came to see him.

"'Ain't seen you up at the club lately, Joe,' he sez.

"'No,' sez Joe shortly.

"'There was a fine argument the night,' sez the pal, 'between Jack Higgins, of Rotherhithe, an' Harry Wagg, of Poplar, on Moonicapel Lan'lordism.'

"'Oh,' sez Joe, very cold.

"'Yes,' sez the pal, 'an' we passed a resolution that nobody should pay rent.'

"'Oh,' sez Joe, very indignant, 'well, that's not my idea of true Socialism,' he sez. 'That's what I call robbery, an' you can tell the secretary to scratch my name orf the club books.'

"'But, Joe!' sez the pal.

"'I'm afraid I can't argue with you,' sez Joe, very firm. 'Me motor-car's at the door, an' I've got to go to a meetin' of property-owners to protest against the new drainage bye-law. Then I've got to go to me solicitor. Them new tenants of mine are complainin' about the roof leakin'. They're a dissatisfied, ungrateful lot,' he sez; 'why, it was only last week I had their backyards whitewashed!'

I must say about Nobby that, havin' sixty odd pounds in his pouch, didn't turn his head. All the way up to London we talked about what we'd do.

"'The great thing,' sez Nobby, 'is not to drink anything till quite late—you can't enjoy yourself if you've got a skinful.'

"The train pulled up outside London, an' people crowded into the carriage. There had been a race meetin', and all the chaps who got in was saying 'Did you ever see such ridin' in your life?' an' 'He ought to have won by the length of a street,' an' 'The jockey pulled his head orf,' an' 'I wish the White Prince had dropped dead,' an' similar light-hearted chatter.

"Then one feller in a big box coat an' buttons as big as saucers took his coat down orf the rack an' folded it on his knees.

"'Gentlemen,' he sez, 'I've had a very good day, an' as I'm anxious to distribute me money for the good of the public, I will endeavour to show you a noo an' original game, invented by the Emp'ror of Germany, entitled, "Can you find the lady?" I have here in me hand three common or ordinary cards, the nine of di'monds, the six of clubs, an' the queen of spades.'

"So he juggles 'em all over the coat, and lays them face down.

' Now,' he sez ' I'll bet any sportsman a sov'reign he can't spot the lady.'

"Before I could stop him, Nobby had a quid in his hand.

"'Here you are,' he sez, an' picked out the queen.

"Anybody can pick out the queen the first time the chap does it, an' me an' Nobby used to make a lot of money at Aldershot Races spottin' the three-card chaps, an' havin' the first penn'orth, so to speak.

"The card chap paid over his quid. an' Nobby put it in his pocket.

"'Now,' sez the card chap, shufflin' the three cards again, 'I'll bet you five pound you can't spot the lady.'

"But Nobby didn't say anything.

"'I'll bet you five pound to three pound you can't spot the lady,' sez the man to Nobby, but Nobby was lookin' out of the winder an' whistlin' thoughtful.

"'Here—you!' sez the card chap, touchin' Nobby's knee, 'you're a sportsman, ain't you? You've won a quid of mine, now, I'll give you another chance.'

"'I never gamble,' sez Nobby, solemn.

"The card chap sort of choked in the throat.

"'You—you,' he gasps, 'why, you won a quid of mine just now.'

"'That wasn't gambling,' sez Nobby, that was a certainty.'

"'D'ye mean to say you ain't goin' to try your luck again?' sez the card chap, very fierce.

"'I do,' sez Nobby.

"'Then gimme back my quid,' sez the card chap, with his eyes bulgin' out.

"'I'll give you a push in the face,' sez Nobby, serious, ' if you ask me for money.'

"The card chap nearly had a fit.

"'Give the man his money,' sez one of his pals.

"But there never was a man in the world who could get money out of Nobby once he got his pay-hooks on it, an' they argued an' argued all the way to London, but Nobby sez nothin', except to pass a few remarks about the card chap's face.

"'I'll wait for you outside the station,' sez the cove.

"'As near the amblance,' sez Nobby, 'as you can get, an' you'd better bring your own doctor.'

"There was a quiet sort of feller satin' in the corner of the carriage, who kept quiet, an' after the card man found that Nobby was no go, he turned to the quiet man, an' offered to bet him that he couldn't find the lady. So the quiet man, bet an' lost, an' bet an' lost again, and that put the card chap in a better humour.

"'It's men like you,' he sez to Nobby, 'that ruin sport—blooming poverty-struck soldier!'

"'This gentleman is a sportsman,' sez the card feller, 'with a sportsman's 'art an' a sportsman's feelin's.'

"'I dessay,' sez Nobby, an' the quiet man grinned.

"When we got to the station, where we was gettin' out, we found the door locked.

"'Here,' sez one of the card chap's pals, 'who locked the door—it wasn't locked when we got in?'

"'I did,' sez the quiet man, an' he beckoned a couple of coppers on the station. An' lo an' behold! the station was full of 'em.

"'A little surprise for you gents,' sez the quiet man. 'There's a police officer in every carriage—I'm one myself—an' we're goin' to make a little haul to-night.'

"When me an' Nobby was watchin' the fellers bein' marched away, Nobby sez—

"'This comes of gamblin', Smithy—let this be a warnin' to you.'

"'What about limericks?' I sez.

"'That's not gamblin'—that's intellects.'

"We had a long argument whether we should go to a real tip-top hotel or whether we should stay at the club.*

[* The Union Jack Club.]

"Nobby knew a high-class hotel in Stamford Street, where you can't get a bed under a shillin' a night, an' some of 'em's two shillin's, so we went there. Then we walked down the Waterloo Road an' bought some civilian clothes, an' had 'em brought back to the hotel. Nobby chose 'em. He's got a rare taste, has Nobby. Yaller boots an' yaller kid gloves, straw hats, an' a white weskit for him, an' a white weskit for me. We got cuffs an' 'dickies,' because Nobby said it was a pity to waste money on shirts.

"As we was comin' back, with a little boy carryin' the parcels behind, Nobby sez: 'Harf a tick,' an' dived into a second-hand jewel shop, where you can buy watches that nearly go, an' unredeemed pledges, an' that sort of thing. He come out again in a minute or so, an' we got back to the hotel.

"What with the salmon an' green tie that Nobby had bought, an' the weskit, I looked a treat, an' I must say that Nobby looked a perfec' gentleman.

"What worried me was the collar an' shirt front. I had to get a knife an' make holes for the studs, an' the way that dickey kept risin' up, first one side, an' then the other, was too cruel. I fastened it down with a pin, but that didn't make no difference. That only made it bulge up in front like a windersill.

"But when I saw Nobby, his collar sat on his neck as though he'd been born in it, as neat an' reglar an' even as possible.

"'How did you do it?' I sez,

"'It's a patent of me own,' sez Nobby, very proud. an' started pullin' on his yaller gloves.

"When we was ready to go out, Nobby sez—

"'Hold hard, Smithy, catch hold of this,' and he pulled out an eyeglass.

"'I've got two,' he sez, 'they've got little bits of wire to help you keep 'em in your eye.'

"'Which eye?' I sez.

"'Any eye,' sez Nobby, very calm, it all depends on what eye it fits.' It took me nearly an hour to get the bloomin' thing to stick, an' only then when I shut the eye it was in.

"We got two very fine meerschaum pipes for a shillin' each—you couldn't tell 'em from real ones—an' a couple of gold-mounted sticks for another two bob, an' we strolled into the Strand.

"There must have been something very takin' about our appearance, because everybody we met turned round an' looked at us.

"'How do we look?' sez Nobby.

"'Fine,' I sez, and I'm bound to admit that I fancied meself a bit.

"'If anybody asks you who you are,' sez Nobby 'you're Lord Smithy an' I'm Sir Nobby de Clark.'

"'Certainly,' I sez.

"We strolled up the Strand, an' saw lots of people waitin' outside a theatre.

"'Let's go in,' sez Nobby, so we joined the crowd.

"We had to wait a bit, an' nobody in the crowd took much notice of us, which annoyed Nobby. He can put on the hawhaw officer's voice very well, can Nobby, so he started.

"'Lord Smithy,' he sez, very loud.

"'Yes, Sir Nob,' I sez.

"'Awfully tejus waitin', ain't it?' he sez, very bored.

"A lot of the people looked round, an' that pleased Nobby.

"'I wish we'd brought our own private box,' sez Nobby.

"There was a chap with whiskers, who was readin' an evenin' newspaper, an' he looks up.

"'If you don't want to wait, don't let us keep you,' he sez, sarcastic.

"'What say?' sez Nobby.

"'I say, if you don't want to wait, don't let us keep you,' sez whiskers.

"'Who is this vulgar person?' sez Nobby.

"'Never mind about that,' sez the whisker-feller, who was one of those chaps who's always lookin' out for a row.

"'Smithy—I mean me lord,' sez Nobby, 'is this person with the creepers a friend of

yours?'

"'No, Sir Nob,' I sez.

"'Then,' sez Nobby, very stern, 'all that I can say to him is, go home an' wash the cobwebs orf your face.'

"The evenin' might have passed off very pleasantly, for we got very nice seats, an' there was a young lady on each side of Nobby, an' he was gettin' on splendid. Then a young feller leant over from the back row an' tapped Nobby on the shoulder.

"'Do you mind changing seats? he sez.

"'What for? ' sez Nobby.

"'I want to sit by those young ladies,' sez the young feller.

"'So do I,' sez Nobby, 'an' I admire your nerve.'

"It appears that one was the young feller's financee, an' the other was his sister, an' the remarks that young chap passed when Nobby bought a big box of sweets between the acts for the financee, was somethin' shockin'.

"When the second act started, an' all the lights went down, Nobby got on splendider than ever. So much to that the young feller got up and touched Nobby again.

"'Are you goin' to give up that seat?' he sez, fierce, and very loud, an' everybody in the theatre sez: 'S-sh—turn him out—silence!'

"'Because,' sez the young feller, gettin' hold of Nobby's collar, 'if you don't, I shall chuck you out!'

"'Leave that collar alone,' sez Nobby, alarmed; 'it's new.'

"In a second the fatal thing was done, an' Nobby's 'dickey' was stickin' out of the top of his weskit.

"Nobby felt the disgrace horrible, an' after he'd hit the young chap once or twice an' a policeman an' a chucker-out had got Nobby outside by the pay-box, I managed to stick it in again for him.

"'It's not bein' chucked out that I mind so much,' sez Nobby, very bitter, but I've got no shirt on under that dickey.'

"'How did you fasten it down, then?' I sez.

"'With two bits of stamp paper,' sez Nobby.

III

"Bein' in London with nothin' to do except to spend money, is very much like bein' on duty linin' the road for a royal percession," said Smithy. "There's thousands of people behind you, pushin' and shovin'. and peekin' up their heads trying to get a peep, and there's you in the front rank, with nothin' to do but to see all the sights an' you're wishin' all the time that you was away carryin' coal or doin' somethin' equally intellectual. Doin' anything you've got to do is the worst thing in the world next to not do n' something you want to do.

"There used to be a chap in ours by the name of Hikey—so called because he was always givin' hisself airs—that used to play the flute like—like what-d'ye-call-him?—an' he used to be practisin' at that flute from mornin' to night. When other fellers was enjoyin' themselves at the wet-bar he used to be playin' 'The Last Rose of Summer' or 'Drink to me only with thine eyes.' He had a piece what he called the

'Moonlight Tomato' wot he used to play when he was on guard at the magazine, an' it got about that the post was 'aunted."

"He 'ad another bit called 'The hark that once tarara's 'alls,' an' what that meant I don't know, but it used to make you want to cry—especially if you'd took a little drink.

"Well, Hikey's playin' got round to the Colonel's ears, and the old man took him, excused him all drills an' put him into the band

"'Let him practise as much as he likes,' sez the Colonel to he bandmaster—so in a manner of speakin' Hikey's life ought to have been one gran' sweet song, as the sayin' is. But what did Hikey do? As soon as he found he hadn't got to practise in his spare time, but 'ad as much time to play his flute as he wanted, he started moanin' an' groanin', an' talked about desertin'! Said it was a dog's life, an' he wished he was dead, an' he hadn't joined the army to be a bloomin' minstrel boy.

"There was another feller by the name of 'Happy Johnson,' who used to spend all his time knittin' socks till he got married. One day there was an awful row at the married quarters, an' 'Happy' got hauled up in front of the C.O. for creatin' a disturbance because his sock wasn't darned.

"'Why didn't you darn 'em yourself?' sez the Commandin' Officer, who knew all about 'Happy.'

"'Wot did she marry me for, sir?' sez 'Happy.'

"'I don't know,' sez the Colonel, 'wasn't quite right in her head, I should say.'

"When a man pays money to do hard work, it's an 'obby; but when he gets paid for it, it's jolly hard work.

"Me an' Nobby thought there wouldn't be anything nicer in the world than bargin' about London, with our pockets full of gold, an' havin' nothin' to do but spend it.

"'I'll bet,' sez Nobby, the second day when we was walkin' up the Strand, 'that if me an' you wanted to buy that cab we could.'

"So we went up to the cabby an' asked him what he wanted for the turn out.

"The cabby looked suspicious, an' told us not to act the goat, but Nobby was so jolly earnest about it, that the cabby told him.

"'There you are,' sez Nobby, an' we walked away leavin' the cabman quite upset.

"After that we went into a shop an' asked the price of a di'mond tirara, because Nobby bet we could afford to buy it, if we wanted. Then we stood in front of a boot shop an' reckoned up that we could buy all the boots in the winder twice over. We got tired of this after a bit, because somehow we never saw anything we really did want to buy, except two framed texts in a little shop in the Charing Cross Road, an' they was only 4s. 6d. each.

"We tried havin' expensive dinners. We had one wot cost nearly half-a-dollar, an' then we had a bottle of wine—very high-class wine it was, too, with three labels—and that cost us another eighteenpence. We had a glass apiece, an' then a bottle of beer to take the taste away.

"'That's wine from the wood,' sez the waiter chap.

"'I know,' sez Nobby. 'I could taste the wood quite plain.'

"On the third day Nobby sez—

"'Smithy, how much do you think we've spent?'

"I knew how much I'd spent, an' told him.

"'Less than a bloomin' quid,' sez Nobby, very bitter. 'Smithy, we oughtn't have money, we don't know how to spend it.'

"That money got on our nerves. We tried hard to spend a parcel that day, we even rode in a taxicab, but the driver was struck honest or somethin', an' only charged the legal fare. We had a bit of grub in a Waterloo Road coffee shop, an' me an' Nobby was walkin' very gloomy towards the bridge when a little kid comes up an' sez—

"' 'Give me a ha'penny, guv'nor.'

"'What for?' sez Nobby, very fierce.

"'To get somethin' to eat,' sez the kid.

"'What do you want to eat for? ' sez Nobby, it'll only make you fat.'

"The kid was slinkin' away, when Nobby called him back.

"'Here's a tanner,' he sez, an' gave him sixpence.

"'Don't make a beast of yourself,' sez Nobby, an' the kid grabbed the sixpence an' started runnin' away, when a bright idea struck Nobby.

"'Here!' he sez, an' called the kid back again. This here little boy was a artful little chap wot thought Nobby was goin' to pinch the tanner back, but Nobby, who's got a wonderful way with wild animals, persuades him to come close.

"'Me an' my friend,' sez Nobby, 'will be back in five minutes, so you go an' tell all the little boys an' girls wot want a tanner to buy grub with to come here an' get it.'

"The little boy didn't believe Nobby, I could see that—but he nipped off, an' Nobby sez very solemn—

"'Would you like to do the Lord Hallin'ton act?' sez Nobby.

"Now I knew all about Lord Hallin'ton, because I'd read it in the papers. How he went round the poor parts of London givin' dinners to poor kids, so I sez—

"'Rather.'

"We went over to a bank an' we got nearly a hundred pounds in tanners.

"My word, it was heavy! Me an' Nobby was bulgin' all over an' weighed down.

"When we got back to where the kid left us there he was with a dozen other little kids.

"Nobby gave 'em a tanner each, an' made 'em swear see-that-wet-see-that-dry that they'd lay it out in grub.

"I don't know how the news got about, but by the time me and Nobby had walked into a side street there was about a hundred thousand kids round us.

"They was yellin' an' shoutin' an' strugglin' to get at us, an' a stout old gentleman forced his way to Nobby an' asked him what the game was. So Nobby told him, an' the old gent larfed like anything.

"'So that's the way a soldier spends his limerick money, is it?' he sez; 'well, go ahead, an' I'll try to keep these youngsters in order.'

"It wanted a bit of doin' an' I was afraid every minute that the p'lice would come up an' stop us. There was lots of loafers in the crowd, but Nobby landed one a dig in the eye, gave a few remarks to the others, and they left, but the tanners went like magic. It was a fine feelin' whilst it lasted, here was me and Nobby feedin' these kids—some of 'em come twice, but Nobby gave 'em a clump or two, an' that stopped that. At last every bloomin' tanner was gone (an' it took a bit of time to persuade 'em it was gone), an' Nobby sez—

"'I didn't think there were so many kids in the world.'

"The fat old gentleman larfed, an' asked me an' Nobby our names, then he shook hands an' went away.

"By the time we'd paid our bill at the hotel and got to the station we had about a quid each left.

"All the fellers in barracks were surprised to see us.

"'Hullo,' sez Spud Murphy, 'spent all your money already?'

"'Yes,' sez Nobby.

"'How?' sez Spud.

"'Drink an' riotchus livin',' sez Nobby.

"'Did you drink much?' sez Spud.

"'We haven't been sober for three days—have we, Smithy?'

"'No,' I sez.

"Spud looked at us very admirin', an' the chaps in the canteen gave us a bit of a reception.

"It was well known in barracks we was back, an' fellers come from all parts—even from the corporals' room—to know what we did with the money.

"So Nobby made up a most disgraceful tale, wot I won't insult you by repeatin', of our carryin's on, an' sat up in bed after lights-out tellin' how we went to parties with dukes an' earls, till the room corporal said if he didn't stop gassin' he'd put him inside.'

"Next mornin', when me an' Nobby was waitin. at the cook-house to draw the coffee, Nobby sez—

"'Smithy, are you sorry you spent that money?'

"'No,' I sez, an' I wasn't.

"'Do you ever want any more?'

"'No,' I sez.

"'Nor me, either,' sez Nobby, 'no more limericks for me.'

"When we got in to breakfast there was a letter waitin' for us. I opened it.

"'Dear sirs,' sez the letter, 'yesterday I had pleasure in witnessing your charity; as you were doing my work, permit me to recompense you.'

"It was signed 'Hallington.'

"'The little fat man!' sez Nobby, with a gasp. 'What's he sent?'

"I opened the cheque ; it was for a hundred pounds!

"'Smithy,' sez Nobby, shakin' his head, 'we'll never get rid of that money! Let's stick to it till flat racin' starts—then I know a way to make it go!'"

## CHAPTER XII

"Noby Clark," explained Private Smith, "has got an uncle who's fairly good. He keeps a ham and beef shop in Lewisham High Road, and naturally, being a bit well off, can afford to be eccentric.

"He's a very fine old chap," said Smithy warmly. "If he gets a side of bacon that's gone off, or a tub of butter a bit high, do you think he throws it away? Not he. He gives it to the pore."

Smithy glowed.

"He sends Nobby lots of letters of advice and tracks, and sometimes he slips in half a dollar in stamps. Nobby is always anxious to get his uncle's letters, but I've known him to have a slice of bad luck for six letters runnin'.

"One mornin' the postman brought a fat letter in. 'Private Clark,' he sez, and Nobby nipped along the barrack-room, but his face fell when he saw how fat the letter was.

"'It's a bit too heavy to be any good,' he sez very bitter, and weighin' the letter in his hand; 'if this is another Straight Talk to Enquirin' Sinners, Smithy, something will 'ave to be done.' He tore open the letter very careful an' took out a printed paper. 'Track.' he sez bitterly, 'a track about drinkin' an' quarrelin'.'

"Then be took out another paper.

"'Track,' he sez bitterer than ever, 'a track about smokin'.'

"Then he took out another paper.

"'Tra—' he stopped, 'no it ain't—here. Smithy, what's this?' Nobby was all of a tremble, an' so was I, for if it wasn't a fiver, a real white crinkly fiver, I've never seen one.

"Nobby was quite shook up an' so was I.

"'Smithy,' sez Nobby, his voice all broke, 'pick up them beautiful tracks that my dear Uncle Joe sent me.'

"'I can't, Nobby,' I sez, 'you chucked 'em on the fire.'

"'Did I—did I?' sez Nobby, horror-struck, 'did I throw away my dear uncle's tracks—did I burn them lovely words—oh, horror!'

"Then one of the fellers chipped in.

"'Spud Murphy's got the one about drink; 'e picked it out of the fireplace, Nobby,' he sez.

"Nobby stood lookin' at the banknote, crinklin' it an' looking at the watermark.

"'Spud Murphy's got no right to my dear uncle's track—but he's welcome to it. I only 'ope,' Nobby went on very solemn, 'that the words in that there track will do him good.'

"There was a letter along with the other goods, and Nobby read it.

"'My dear nephew,' read Nobby. 'This comes hopin' to find you—um—um—um. I am glad to hear you go regularly to—um—um, but am sorry to hear you are ashamed to go to the meetin's because you've got no money to put in the plate.... Can quite understand it.... I don't see why you should wait till I die before getting some of my money, so as a reward... I am sendin' you ten pounds.'

"'What,' I sez, an' Nobby read it again. 'Ten pound,' he sez, an' pulled the banknote out of his pocket to examine it. It was 'Five' right enough as plain as plain. 'I promise to pay,' etc.

"'Dear uncle's made a mistake,' sez Nobby, all trembly, or else the other five is comin' on.' He turned the envelope inside out, but there was nothin' in it.

"'Go on with the letter,' I sez.

"'... Ten pounds,' read Nobby slowly, but certain persons havin' said that you don't read my little tracks—' Nobby stopped and went white.

"'Go on,' I sez.

"'Certain persons havin' said you don't read my tracks nor my letters either, I—have—put—the—other—five—pound—'

"Nobby sort of collapsed on to the nearest bed-cot.

"'Where?' I sez.

"'Between the last two pages of the track on drink an' quarrelin',' he sez, in a holler voice.

"I tell you," said Smithy seriously, "it shook me an' Nobby up a bit, but bimeby Nobby pulls hisself together and jumps up. 'Smithy,' he sez, 'that low feller Spud has got my dear uncle's track wot he sent to me—I want to read that track; it'll do me more good than Spud. Where is he?'

"Then somebody said he'd seen Spud going over to the canteen, so me an' Nobby run as hard as we could to find him.

"Sure enough there he was, but our 'earts went down into our number nines when we saw him—he was sittin' by hisself drinking lemonade and looked very sad.

"'Cheer-o, Spud,' sez Nobby, in a chokin' voice. 'How goes it? What are you drinkin'?'

"Spud shook his head sorrerfully.

"'I've given up the cursed drink,' he sez, in a humble voice.

"'Since when?' sez Nobby, very loud. 'Since when, you low hypocrite?'

"Spud didn't take no offence. He only sighed.

"'Since reading your dear Uncle Joe's track,' he sez.

"'Spud,' sez Nobby, droppin' his voice an' shakin' Spud by the hand, 'Spud, you make me feel ashamed of meself. Perhaps I ought to give it up, too; perhaps them beautiful words might be the makin' of me; let's have a look at my uncle's track wot I lent you.'

"'Wot you chucked away,' sez Spud, very gentle.

"'Wot happened to slip out of my hand an' was picked up by a low thief who happened to be passin',' sez Nobby, very ferocious, but managed to get hisself under control again; 'so, therefore, dear Spud, let me have a dekko at them lovely words.'

"'I haven't quite finished with it yet,' sez Spud, sippin' his lemonade and smacking his lips. This is the stuff to drink, Nobby. If I'd read your uncle's track earlier I might have been pounds in pocket.'

"I thought Nobby would have a fit. He got red in the face an' he gnashed his teeth.

"'Spud,' he sez, after a bit, 'Spud, old feller, are you goin' to see a comrade continue on what I might call the down grade without raisin' a hand to help him? And any way,' he went on, gettin' wilder and wilder, 'it's my bloomin' track; it was sent to me by my dear Uncle Joe, an' if you don't hand it over, I'll give you a wipe on the jaw.'

"All the fellers in the canteen began to gather round on the off chance of a fight.

"'Wot's up, Nobby?' sez Fatty Green, a very nice young feller with a curly head.

"'This perishing recruit's got a track of mine,' roars Nobby, pullin' off his coat, 'a beautiful track about drinkin' an' quarrellin', an' won't hand it over, so I'm goin' to knock his head off.'

"'Give the man his track,' sez Fatty, who was an off-an'-on teetotaller, an' all the other fellers said the same.

"Things looked a bit rough-housish when suddenly the bugle sounded orf for 'orderly men,' an' Nobby staggered back.

"'That's me,' he sez, an' I felt sorry for him. In a manner of speakin' he was tore between love an' duty, as the song sez.

"'Smithy,' he whispers to me, 'I've got to go and draw the groceries; keep your eye on this blighter an' don't let him out of your sight.'

"When Nobby had gone I sez to Spud—

"'Spud, me lad—I want a few words with you.'

"'Ave 'em here,' sez Spud, sippin' his lemonade, but I took his arm an' walked him down to the back field, where there was nobody about.

"'Spud,' I sez kindly, hand over Nobby's uncle's track.'

"'For why?' sez Spud, looking round for some one to take his part.

"'If you ain't enough of a gentleman to understand that when a feller gets a private track from his uncle he don't want nobody else to read it, I can't explain,' I sez. Just then Nobby came runnin' back from the parade ground, 'avin' got another feller to draw the groceries.

"'Come on,' he sez, an' so we gave Spud a number two jujitsu push.

"'You hold his legs, Smithy,' sez Nobby, who was sittin' on Spud's head; 'now, you mouldy highway robber, where's that track?'

"'Lemme get up,' sez Spud, strugglin', but Nobby went carefully through his pockets.

"'Here it is,' he yells, an' pulls out the paper. Sure enough, snug between the last two leaves was the other fiver.

"'I'll report this,' sez Spud, when we let him up.

"'Do,' sez Nobby, very cheerful, 'do.'"

CHAPTER XIII

THE BAA-LAMB

The Army is a queer place, and soldiers really do extraordinary things. Once there was a martinet colonel of the Anchester Regiment who was known at the War Office as a "strong man," and once or twice his portrait crept into the pages of illustrated papers. As a matter of fact, he was not a strong man at all, but a bullying, brow-beating, terrorising weakling, with a taste for whisky and bridge. Also he was a bad loser, and collected postage stamps. And if that description isn't enough to damn any man, I should like to know what is.

When the general came round on his annual inspection he remarked that there was a great deal of crime in the regiment, and the colonel spoke vaguely of discipline and the standard of recruiting, and after that the inspection was more "military" than ever.

The colonel used to live out of barracks, and one guest night he was driving to mess along a dark country road, and his horse took a tumble, and the colonel picked himself out of the road with a broken head and his features fairly well displaced. Then he discovered a fine wire stretched across the road, and knew that it constituted the regiment's vote of censure.

A few days later, as he was sitting at dinner, a heavy flint stone crashed through the window and all but brained him. So the colonel took the hint and went on half pay. During the war, the supply of ' strong men" having run short, owing to the lamentable miscalculation which led them to match their strength against big, fat kopjes, the War Office sent for the colonel, and made him first a brigadier-general, then a local major-general. They gave him a brigade, which, to his—and its—intense annoyance, included the Anchester Regiment.

The general had many narrow escapes from death before he returned to England, "on account of ill-health," and he now lives near Farnborough, and spends his days explaining why the Boers cut him up at Veltfontein, capturing his two pompoms and decimal nine-nine-nine of his convoy. His friends call him "Mad Jack," and he rather likes the nickname, because there has grown about the title a legend of recklessness in danger which he does not object to at all. As a matter of fact, his madness took the form of losing his head on the slightest provocation and calling for help in a loud voice.

I am particularly concerned with this retired general, because he writes a great deal to the newspapers, nowadays, demanding that the Great General should be recalled from Babuland to "sweep the something stables of our rotten War Office, and reduce order from the chaos, etc."

Now this is not a bad wheeze at all. For once upon a time, before the Great General went to Babuland, an obscure captain of infantry wrote ecstatic letters to the newspapers of that delightful country, acclaiming the Great General as the greatest kind of Great General that ever was. And when the Great General arrived he sought out the obscure captain of infantry and made him a colonel on the staff, which everybody in Babuland knows, and talks about.

Now Smithy—Private Smith, as ever is—of the aforesaid Anchester Regiment, and I have had many earnest talks about the Army and the War Office and Mr. Haldane; and when we have been in any kind of doubt we have summoned to our council Private Clark, whose other name is Nobby.

"The Army is a queer place, and soldiers do funny things," said Smithy, shaking his head wisely. "You take the ordinary soldier an' start talkin' music-hall-soldier talk to him, an' likely as not he'll dot you one. A soldier hates bein' called a hero—when he's sober—an' fellers I know would go miles out of their way sooner than hear some fat-headed civilian talkin' about the dear old flag. Chaps mostly enlist because they're hard up, as everybody knows. Some chaps enlist because they have a row with their people.

"'When are you goin' to do some work, Bob?' sez the old man.

"'Next week,' sez Bob.

"'So you said this time last year,' sez the old man, an' if you think it's goin' to keep you through another flat racin' season, you're mistook.'

"With that Bob gets despondent.

"'I can't get no work,' he sez, very bitterly. 'I've been sittin' in front of the fire for the last week schemin' and thinkin' an' plannin', an' that's all the thanks I get!'

"'Why don't you go out and look for it,' sez the old man, at five in the mornin'—same as me?'

"'What!' sez Bob, very indignant, 'me go out in the mornin', riskin' double pneumatics, an' all! I'm ashamed of you father.'

"'I do it,' sez the old man.

"'You're older,' sez Bob, 'an' in a manner of speakin' 'ardened. I don't know what I'll do! I've a good mind to commit suicide!'

"'Why don't you go for a soldier?' sez the father, 'it's a nice lazy life—just suit you!'

"That sets the chap thinkin', an' before a week's past he's took the oath to serve his Majesty the King, 'is heirs, an' successors, an' the generals an' officers set over him, so help me, etcetra.

"His mother cries, an' sez he's disgraced the family, an' all his sisters start yappin', an' his little brother asks him to bring him home a sword or two, an' the old man breathes in a light-hearted way, an' sez that doin' nothing for seven years'll make a man of him.

"Pore feller! When he gets to the depot, an' is kicked out of bed at 5 a.m., an' made to clean hisself an' turn out on a square that ain't been properly warmed, he wakes up out of his trance.

"There's only two chaps I know that ever come into the army for glory, an' one was off his head an' the other was Conky Barlam. We used to call him 'Baa-Lamb,' owin' to his simple ways. He was, indeed, the simplest feller I've ever clapped eyes on. A perfec' child he was, an' always talkie about the 'dear ole regiment,' an' the 'glorious Anchesters,' an' was one of them chaps that's always energetic in doin' the wrong thing. Made up a song he did, an' the first verse went

The noblest regiment on this earth

That's always makin' stirs,

It is that corps of stirlin' worth

What's called the Anchesters.

"He used to volunteer for duty—would have gone on guard seven days a week if they'd let him—an' actually paraded before the colonel an' asked if he could see the reg'mental relics!

"We've got a lot—what with flags we've taken, an' stuff we've looted in various wars, an' the officers' mess is full of diamond-hilted swords an' gold saucepans, an' things that our illustrious officers have pinched from the hateful foe from time to time.

"The colonel was very pleased at Baa-Lamb's sauce, for the officers are as proud as Punch of the trophies, an' he actually took Baa-Lamb round an' showed him everything hisself!

"I was at the orderly room an' heard the colonel tell the adjutant.

"'By the way, Umfreville, that new recruit of "B" Company—Barlam's his name, I think—is a singularly intelligent feller. Took a tremendous interest—an intelligent interest—in the trophies—his father was a collector in a small way, an' the boy seems to have a fair idea of the value of our things.'

"'Yes, sir,' sez the adjutant, who don't hold with soldiers knowin' a 'fair knowledge' of anything, except marchin' an' shootin'.

"Old Baa-Lamb was fair cracked about the flags, an' the swords an' the relics gen'rally.

"'It made my heart swell,' he sez, 'to see them glorious trophies of many a stricken field,' he sez, where our noble officers have gone forth to victory or death,' he sez, 'or both. It makes my heart swell,' he sez, 'to see how them brave fellers have stormed palaces an' always,' he sez, 'gone straight to the place where the expensive loot was. It makes my heart swell—'

"'Dry up,' sez Nobby, or I'll make your eye swell!'

"'But think of them noble fellers,' sez Baa-Lamb, excited, 'amidst cannon roar an' flyin' shot—'

"'Get out!' sez Nobby, very disgusted.

"What pleased Baa-Lamb best was when he found a rhyme for 'di'mond-hilted sword,' an' wrote a little poem about it.

Our officers, they bravely led
The privates through the breach,
An' found the enemy had fled
Out of their lawful reach.
Ah! many a high an' stilted lord
That day exclaimed, 'Great Scot!
I've lost my di'mond-hilted sword
An' golden mustard pot!'

"You must understand that we sort of put up with Baa-Lamb because he was such a simple josser an' very kind-hearted. So when one mornin' me an' Nobby woke up an' found him missin' an' his bed not been slept in, we felt sorry for him, for the colonel's awfully down on chaps who overstay their leave, an' the night before old Baa-Lamb had gone out into town to meet his 'dear uncle' what had come down from London to see him.

"As a matter of fact, we didn't feel sorry very long, because it was soon all over barracks that Baa-Lamb had gone for good—an' so had the di'mond-hilted sword an' several other valuables wot he'd written poems about"

CHAPTER XIV

NOBBY'S DOUBLE

"You might say that soldiers have got most of the vices," said Private Smith, "because they're ordinary men. Most fellers have got a large whack of vice concealed about 'em, it don't matter what they are, I once knew a school-board officer who went round the country on his holiday as 'Old Bill Maggit of Bermondsey' what would fight anybody at twelve stone, an' I knew a quiet young feller who always put on a clean white shirt every Sunday, who's now doin' five years for robbery an' violence. We're all bad, but most of us are afraid of the police. When you find a chap who don't give two pennorth of sugar for the biggest copper that ever told a lie, you can bet he's going to be a criminal, because he don't possess the only thing what keep, people honest—and that's the fear of bein' found out.

"But whatever you say about soldiers, you can't say they bet. They play banker, an' nap, an fives,' an' pontoon,* an' lose fab'lous sums. But they don't bet, except very rarely. When they do happen to bet, it's a bad thing for the bookie. Close by Anchester there's a racin' stable, and from what me an' Nobby heard, there was a horse in that stable by the name of Mutton Pie what couldn't lose the Manchester Handicap.

*[* Vingt-et-un (blackjack).]*

"One of the stable lads was down at the canteen last Sunday an' said that Mutton Pie would be passin' the winnin' post when the other horses were scratchin' their heads an' wonderin' where he'd gone. Everybody in Anchester was on Mutton Pie, an' a lot of chaps in the regiment, too. Me an' Nobby was on to the extent of five bob each way.

"What made us fancy him so much was his intelligence. He was in a race once at Hurst Park; there was only four runners, an' every one of the others could beat him. So what did the noble horse do? Why, when he was at the startin' post he up an' kicks the favourite in the ribs. Then he kicked the jockey off the second favourite. That brought the field down to two, an' the other one would have won, only just before they got to the winnin' post Mutton Pie stretched his head round an' bit the other horse s ear off. So Mutton Pie won by a head an a bit of an ear he had in his mouth.

"'That's the horse for me,' sez Nobby, 'he'll win, if he ain't poisoned before the day.'

"The day before the race there was great excitement in barracks. That afternoon, when we were listening to a chap in 'H,' who was tellin' us that Mutton Pie hadn't got an earthly, an' that Jubilee was chucked into the race, the adjutant's orderly came in an' said that the adjutant wanted to see me.

"'Me?' I sez, astonished.

"'You,' sez the orderly, 'and look nippy.'

So I doubled across to the orderly room.

"'Ah, Smith,' sez the adjutant, I want you to do something for me.'

"'Yes, sir,' I sez, wonderin' what was in the wind.

"'There's a boy joinin' the regiment, the son of the late Sergeant-Major Stevens.'

"'Yes, sir,' I sez.

"'The boy's got a stepfather, an anarchist or socialist, or something, who doesn't want the boy to join.'

"He waited a bit, an' I waited a bit.

"'Well,' he sez, carelessly, 'if you an' your friend Clark should run across this man—he's an awful brute from what I hear—I want you to treat him kindly.'

"'Yes, sir,' I sez, 'I will, sir.'

"'Don't hurt him,' he sez.

"'No, sir,' I sez.

"He looks hard at me.

"'Do you understand?' he sez, and winks just like that.

"'I wasn't long givin' Nobby the office. Afterwards we went up to the room to tea, an' we was half-way through when there was a knock at the door. Nobody knocks at a barrack-room door, so we knew it was a civilian.

"'Come in,' everybody shouted at once.

"The door opens, an' in walked the finest kind of blighter you've ever seen in your natural. He wore a big black hat an' a red necktie, with egg marks. His hair was long, an' his face was one of them oily faces that always shines. He looks round the room an' sniffs.

"'Do you want anybody?' sez Nobby, very polite.

"He sniffs again.

"'Or a handkerchief?' sez Nobby.

"The oily chap didn't take any notice of what Nobby said.

"'So this,' he sez, 'is a barrack-room. An' these are the licensed butchers what the likes of me pay taxes for.'

"'The butcher's out just now,' sez Nobby, 'owin' to his havin' an appointment down town to meet a girl.'

"The oily chap looks at Nobby very scornful.

"'Come here, my man,' he sez haughtily.

"Nobby walks up to him.

"'Do you know who I am?' he sez.

"'Do I get a prize for guessin'?' sez Nobby.

"'I'm one of your masters,' sez the oily chap,

"'Go on,' sez Nobby.

"'I keeps you,' sez the chap.

"'Who keeps you?' sez Nobby.

"'The sweat of me brow,' sez the chap.

"Nobby looks at his oily dial.

"'Well you ought to be well off,' sez Nobby.

"The chap looked very fiercely at Nobby.

"'I'll have you understand,' he began, when in walked a kid.

"He was one of the nicest little kids you ever saw, with yallar hair an' eyes like china saucers.

"'Ha,' sez the oily chap, jumpin' forward an' catchin' the kid by the arm. 'You're the boy I'm lookin' for.'

"'Hold on,' I sez, what's the game?'

"The oily chap turned on me with a haughty look.

"'Don't interfere,' he sez, 'this boy's my son, an' was goin' to disgrace hisself by joinin' the army.'

"The boy was strugglin' to get his arm away.

"'Wait a bit,' sez Nobby, 'look after the door Smithy. Before we go any further, Face, I would like to ask you a civil question.'

"'What's that?' sez the oily chap.

"'It's this,' sez Nobby slowly. Would you prefer goin' out of this room by the door, or would you prefer to be chucked out of the winder—there's only two ways?"

"'What d'ye mean?' sez the oily chap, lookin' scared.

"'Years an' years ago,' sez Nobby, 'I was kidnapped by gipsies because of me good looks—did you make any remark?'

"'No' sez the oily chap.

"'It's a good job for you you didn't,' sez Nobby, 'the chap what kidnapped me had a face like yours, only not so bad, an I promised me Uncle Bill when be died, that if ever I met you I'd do you in.'

"' "Nobby," sez my Uncle Bill, "don't hurt the poor feller." "I won't, uncle!" I sez. "Let his end be painless" "It shall, Uncle Bill," I sez. "Don't do it with an hammer, but just drop him gently out of a winder," sez my Uncle Bill, an' that's what I'm goin' to do,' sez Nobby.

"'You'll get into trouble for this threat, me man,' sez the oily chap, who was frightened to death.

"'I know I will,' sez Nobby sadly. 'A fortune-teller told me so. "You'll be charged with murder," she sez, "but you'll get off as soon as the jury has seen a photo of the feller you've killed."'

"I don't know how long this sort of thing would have gone on, but we heard a sword clinking in the passage outside, an' stood to attention as Captain Umfreville, the adjutant, came into the barrack-room He looked at the kid an' looked at the oily chap.

"'What's wrong?' he sez.

"'This—this scoundrel,' splutters the oily chap, pointin' to Nobby, 'has dared to threaten me! By heavens, sir, I'll have the law on you—'

"'Me?' sez Nobby, astonished. 'What for?'

"'Didn't you say—?

"'If I've opened me mouth,' sez Nobby in a shocked voice, 'except to pass the time of day, may I be blowed.'

"'What are you doing with that boy?' sez the adjutant.

"'My son,' sez the oily chap,

"'Your stepson,' sez the officer.

"'What's it to do with you?' sez the oily chap with a snort. 'Am I a free citizen to be talked to by a gilded nincompoop?'

"'I'm neither a nincompoop, nor am I particularly gilded,' sez the adjutant quietly, 'and if you cannot behave yourself, I will have you put outside. Again I ask you what you are doing with that boy?'

"'I'm taking him home,' sez the oily bird. 'I know the law as well as you, Mr. Blooming officer, and the law sez I can take him.'

"By the look in Umfreville's face I could see Greasy knew what he was talkin' about.

"'Very good,' sez the officer, 'you may take him.'

"'What, sir,' sez Nobby, 'are you goin' to allow a lobster like that—'

"'Be quiet, Clark,' sez the officer, ' you can take the boy, Mr.—'

"'Snieff,' sez the oily chap.

"'You may take the boy, Mr. Snieff, after I have made a few inquiries; in the meantime you may remain here if you wish.'

"'I'm not goin' to leave this den of iniquity till I leave with this young varmint,' sez Snieff.

"'Unless you can produce very excellent reasons why it should not be so, the boy will be sworn in tomorrow,' sez the captain.

"'Don't you worry,' sez Snieff, 'I'll produce reasons, an', what's more, I'll be there to see 'em enforced.' An' when the officer walked out of the room Snieff walked out behind him.

"We watched him strollin' about the square an' tried to lure him into the barrack-room, but it wasn't any go. After a bit he walked down into the field.

"'Smithy,' sez Nobby, 'how would you like twenty-one days' C.B.?'

"'About as much as I would like a kick in the back,' I sez.

"'I've got an idea,' sez Nobby.

"If I was a writin' chap like you, an' had to write a story about what happened to the oily chap in the back field (behind the Gymnasium where nobody could see), I think I'd start off like this: 'When the shades of night were fallin' fast, Smithy an' Nobby might have been seen carryin' a bundle, viz., the oily chap.'

"We got him over the wall at the back an' on to the footpath. A little way along we found Pug Wilson an' Spud Murphy with a barrer.

"'I'm goin' to tie the sack up,' sez Nobby, an' if you make a sound I'll knock your bloomin' head off.

"We got him through the town, by side streets, an' wheeled the barrer to the goods yard of the railway station.

"'It's all right,' Nobby sez. 'They're goin' to put an empty carriage on, an' I've found out which one it is.'

"We carried the oily chap along, over the rails, till we come to the carriage. It was a sort of horse-box, but there was a little compartment at the end for the stable-boy. We took Snieffy out of the sack an' tied his hands, an' shoved him through an openin' in the compartment into the horse-box itself. Then we got out an' strolled on to the platform. There was a lot of people waitin' to see Mutton Pie off to Manchester, and by and by they shunted another horse-box on to the train.

"'What's that for?' sez Nobby, to make sure.

"'It's an empty we're sendin' to Manchester,' sez a porter.

"Nobby kept an anxious eye on Snieff's box, an' when the whistle blew an' the train started to move somebody sez—

"'What's that scufflin' noise?'

"'It's only Mutton Pie,' sez Nobby.

"'But I heard a feller shoutin',' sez the chap.

"'Three cheers for Mutton Pie!' yells Nobby. 'Shout, Smithy,' he whispers, 'or they'll hear him.'

"So we all yelled together, an' the people on the platform joined in, as the train ran out of the station.

"'Where's the first stop?' sez Nobby.

"' Manchester,' sez the porter.

"'Good,' sez Nobby.

"'Have you backed Mutton Pie?' sez the porter

"'Well,' sez Nobby, 'I've done what you might call a double.'"

## CHAPTER XV

THE FIGHTING ANCHESTERS

Once upon a time Smithy and Nobby Clark "put a bit in the papers" for their own immediate profit and glorification. The "bit" they put in was a gross libel, and the unfortunate editor had to apologise and pay £20 to a local hospital, but Smithy and Nobby got half a guinea for the "information," so that they were not greatly perturbed over the editor's downfall. But in a roundabout way the Colonel of the 1st Anchesters came to hear of the part his two men had played, and acted accordingly. Since when both Nobby and Smithy have retired permanently from journalism.

I was reminded of this unpleasant episode by Smithy himself, who has recently been acting the part of mediator between Pug Wilson and Big Harvey. It would appear that the said Pug Wilson did wrongly and improperly describe the said Big Harvey as a "cellar-flapping gaol-bird," thereby bringing the said Big Harvey into ridicule and contempt; and, moreover, of his envy, hatred, and malice this said Pug Wilson used threatening and abusive language to the said Big Harvey, calculated thereby to cause a breach of the King's peace.

"I don't know what's coming over the Army," said Smithy in despair. "There used to be a time when if a feller called another feller a liar, he had to go through it on the spot. To call a feller a thief was to ask for a plunk in the eye, and when one feller cast reflections on another feller's family it used to take six men an' a bugler to pry 'em apart.

"But they're improving the Army nowadays. We're tryin' to get a superior class of young chaps who can write with both hands and do sums with his feet. Were gettin' men who call their girls 'young ladies,' and sound their h's, and when there's any kind of trouble going cheap these are the fellers that talk about reporting you to the company officer, or else takin' you into court to make you prove your words.

"There's two fellers in 'H' Company who are the limit. One of 'em calls himself Vane, and used to drive his own motor-car before he came down in the world. Nobby sez it was a motor-'bus, and that old Vane lost his job because his face frightened the horses, and the 'bus got the blame.

"The other feller's name's Antony Gerrard, Esquire (that's that he put on his attestation paper), and nobody knows what he was. We thought we'd found out once. But when it came to the pinch, the police couldn't recognise him, and although the lady said she was almost sure that that was the man who took her watch, Antony Gerrard, Esquire, got off.

"I've often been sorry that I'm not in 'H.' it's almost worth the disgrace of belonging to the worst shooting company in the battalion to hear these fellers talk to each other.

"All the room stands round and listens.

"'Well, Tony, dear boy,' sez Vaney, 'you and I are for guard to-morrow.'

"'Horrid grind,' sez Antony Gerrard, Esquire.

"'Beastly bore,' sez Vaney.

"'The whole system's rotten,' sez Antony Gerrard, Esquire, disgustedly. 'The economic wastage—'

"'And the undisputed shrinkage.' sez Vaney.

"'True, true,' sez Antony Gerrard, Esquire, musingly, 'all these factors count in the consideration of the vital principle.'

"Sometimes these two fellers fall out. 'Specially on pay nights. Vaney can't take much to drink. Two pints makes him cry, three pints makes him insultin', but fifty bloomin' pints wouldn't make him fight.

"Antony Gerrard, Esquire gets insultin' at the first pint, but bein' a very careful man, he keeps his mouth shut till he sees Vaney.

"The other night both of 'em was in the canteen, and Vaney had just finished his insultin' pint, when Antony Gerrard, Esquire, called him.

"'Vane,' he sez haughtily; 'Vane, you low hound, come here!'

"Vane puts down his pot with a terrible look in his eye, and walks across.

"'Did I hear you speak, you bounder-man?' he sez fiercely.

"'You did,' sez Antony Gerrard, Esquire; 'that is if your ears are as big as your mouth—motor-'bus driver.'

"Vaney pauses a bit an' then sez—

"'Gerrard, you are a low cad.'

"'Be careful what you're sayin', "bus-man," sez Antony Gerrard, Esquire.

"'You're a shockin' low cad—watch-snatcher,' sez Vaney, very pale.

"This brings Antony Gerrard, Esquire, to his feet.

"'Say that expression again,' he says, poking his face in Vaney's. 'Say it again and I will tear you limb from limb—hound.'

"'You would? '

"'I would.'

"'Try it.'

"'Say it again.'

"Vaney gets very pale, and so does Antony Gerrard, Esquire.

"'By heavens,' sez Antony Gerrard, Esquire, grindin' his teeth, 'I've killed better men than you, Vane, for less than what you've said.'

"'Kill me,' sez Vane, very faint; 'kill me, I dare you!'

"'You low, coarse sweep,' sez Antony Gerrard Esquire in a trembling voice.

"Nobby was sittin' close alongside when they was carryin' on this conversation. Nobby was tellin' a feller a yarn about a rich uncle who had a tailor's shop in Deptford, an' was warmin' up to it. This talk of Vaney's and Antony Gerrard, Esquire's, got on his nerves, so he looks up.

"'Touch me at your peril,' Vaney was sayin'.

"'Cad,' sez the other chap.

"Nobby chipped in—

"'If you two fellers don't shut up, I'll plug both of you so that you'll wish you was never born.'

"'Can't two gentlemen have a dispute without a third party intervenin'?' sez Vane haughtily.

"'No, they can't' sez Nobby, 'and if you call me a third party I'll smash you.'

"That's the argument that always settles them two. My experience is that fellers in this world ain't doubly gifted. If a chap can run he can't jump; if he can talk he can't fight, and vicer verser. Bill Mason is the worst talker in the battalion. Chaps who don't know him get a wrong impression.

"Vaney tried him once. Gave him a bit of cheek, and waited to see what he'd do. Bill didn't do anything, and didn't say anything, so Vaney went on.

"'What's that you call me?' sez Bill, after a bit.

"'A lout,' sez Vaney.

"'What's a lout?' sez Bill.

"'A lout,' sez Vaney, is a low, ignorant—'

"'All right,' sez Bill, 'I've got your meanin', and Vaney went down on the floor with a bang that shook two windows out of the room. But fellers like Bill Mason are gettin' scarcer and scarcer. Now and again we get a man into the regiment who's a bit of a surprise.

"Just after we came home from India, years an' years ago, a new recruit came from the depot. He was a nice quiet chap, who didn't say much to anybody. Drank his pint with the rest of us; made no friends, and took no liberties. He was a good clean soldier, and that's the sort of chap we like. Lots of fellers tried him on, but it was no catch, He'd got a way of turning things off with a joke. I think he must have been something decent before he joined the Army, and Antony Gerrard, Esquire, said that anybody could see he was a gentleman.

"The new feller's name was Gordon—or that's what he called himself. Antony Gerrard, Esquire, tried to chum on to him.

"'By the way, old feller,' he sez one day, 'are you any relation to the Gordons of Loch Lomond?'

"Gordon looks at him with a quiet smile.

"'No, I'm not,' he sez, 'I'm a first cousin to the Gordon Highlanders.'

"That shut up Antony Gerrard, Esquire; he couldn't think of any repartee for ten minutes, an' then Gordon had gone.

"Nobby had toothache one day, and was a bit short in his temper, and somehow or other got foul of Gordon. Nobby has got a nasty tongue when so inclined, and what he said to Gordon meant fighting.

"Gordon was as quiet as anything.

"'I'll fight you, he said, 'but I'm not going to fight a man with jaw ache.'

"Nobby thought he was funking it, but as soon as Nobby's tooth stopped aching a day or two after, the pair went down into the back fields to settle the matter.

"Nobby came into the canteen, and I could tell by the look of his face that he'd fallen on something.

"'Hullo!' I sez, 'had your fight?'

"Nobby looked out of one eye an' nodded.

"'Yes,' he sez; then, after a bit, 'I'm sorry the toothache didn't last a little longer,' he sez mournfully.

"When Gordon came in he looked pleased with hisself, and that ruffled me, because I was fond of old Nobby.

"'Look here, Gordon,' I sez, in a bit of a huff, 'you needn't grin at what you've done to Nobby.'

"It was the only time I've known Gordon to get cross.

"'I'm not grinning, Smithy,' he sez. 'If you want to know why my mouth's this shape, ask your friend Nobby.'

"We all lived together in love and harmony for a long time after this. Sometimes fighting used to run through a regiment like measles through a bloomin' orphan school, but that time seems all gone past. We were gettin' down to Antony Gerrard, Esquire's class—we were 'orribly desperate talkers. That's what I said before. I don't suppose it's the fault of the Army; the country's to blame.

"Nobody fights nowadays unless he's drunk. We was discussing it the other night in the canteen. The question rose over a question of tuppence wot Big Harvey said Pug Wilson owed him.

"One thing led to another, and Pug got a bit personal.

"'Well,' sez Nobby to Big Harvey, 'I wouldn't let a man say a thing like that about my nose if I was you, Big 'un.'

"'I'll make him prove his words,' sez Big Harvey.

"'Why not knock his bloomin' head orf?' suggested Nobby, who likes to see things settled one way or the other.

"'Not me,' said Big Harvey, 'I wouldn't bemean myself.'

"'Well,' sez Nobby, 'bemean him.'

"'Not me,' sez Big Harvey, who's big enough to eat Pug Wilson. 'I don't believe in hittin' a man wot ain't my size.'

"'Don't you worry,' sez Pug, 'there won't be so much of you by the time I've finished with you.'

"I don't know what else was said, because I only stayed an hour an' I didn't hear the end of it.

"Me and Nobby was going out of barracks that evening, as it was Saturday night. We got out intc the High Street when Nobby told me what he thought about things in general.

"'The Army ain't what it used to be, Smithy,' he sez, 'we're gettin' a bit too polite—there ain't none o' the old spirit left wot there used to be. Why, Happy Johnson told me the other day that he thought scrappin' was low an' vulgar, an' George Booth sez a man who strikes another feller is worse than the beasts of the field.'

"Poor old Nobby was quite downhearted about it. I had not noticed it so much myself till Nobby pointed it out.

"Nobby thought it was all owin' to the bad effect of Antony Gerrard, Esquire, and was for takin' him out of his bed one night an chuckin' him in the river.

"We got milder an' milder, an' louder an' louder, and when the regiment went down to Aldershot for the summer manoeuvres it got quite a scandal. They called us the 'Talking Hundred and Tenth,' an' said our motto was, 'All say an' no do.'

"We was brigaded with another regiment, the Royal Wigshire Light Infantry, the dirtiest regiment in the British Army, an' it got a bit too thick when these fellers started chipping up. As we went through their lines they used to shout 'Mama!' an' things like that.

"One of the Wigshires came over into our camp one night an' said he was the light-weight champion of the Army, an' would give any feller a bob who could stand up to him for ten minutes.

"We had got into such a shocking state of peacefulness that nobody said a word, and the Wigshire chap went swaggerin' back to his lines larfin'.

"That night four of us was comin' back to camp.

"There was me and Nobby and Bill Mason and Gordon. We was takin' a short cut through the Wigshires' lines, when one of their chaps spied us an' a feller came up an' very politely asked us to go into their canteen an' have a drink.

"We all went in, an' I could see there was a bit of a lark on.

"'They've gone to get you your drink' sez the feller who asked us in, an' I could see him wink at his pals.

"'There's goin' to be a rough house,' I whispers to Nobby.

"'There is,' sez Nobby.

"A man came along with four cans.

"'Drink hearty,' he sez, with a grin.

"I looked in the can, an' saw it was milk.

"'It's only condensed milk,' he sez, still grinnin', 'but it's good enough.'

"None of our fellers so much as batted an eyelid.

"Nobby looked at the can, and when the laughin' died down, he sez—

"'Friends an' comrades all, I'm goin' to give you a toast.'

"Then I loosened my belt, for I knew that an Orangeman's beanfeast was a tea party compared with the little affair that was coming along.

"'Friends an' comrades,' sez Nobby, 'here's the health of the gallant Wigshires what run away at the Battle of Modderfontein an' left their officers to die.'

"He drank the milk with one eye on the men.

"There was a dead silence for a minute, then the whole crowd jumped at us with a yell.

"But they didn't meet the kind of fellers they expected. Nobby was out for blood, an' Bill Mason was hitting like a steam engine. I did my little bit, an' so did Gordon, who's got a lovely short-arm jab that's worse than lockjaw to the man he hits.

"But there was too many of 'em for us; they came rushin' into the canteen from every part of the camp.

"They drove us back to the counter an' started throwin' things. Then when the situation was gettin' pretty hot, I heard a yell outside, and in came the Anchesters, with belts an' billets of wood, an' anything they could lay their hands on. An', best of all, the first feller to chuck himself into the thick of the fight, yellin' like a lunatic, was Antony Gerrard, Esq., as ever was! The Wicks' didn't wait for a lickin'. They run like they did at Modder.

"Somebody shouted 'Get back to our lines!' an' then we heard the 'General Assembly' sound.

"Antony Gerrard, Esq., had got a whack on the head with a belt, an' was a bit dizzy, but me an' Nobby took an arm each, an' got him home.

"It got into the papers, 'Military Riot at Aldershot,' an' that sort of thing, but, as Nobby said, it was worth the scandal. It made a man of Antony Gerrard, Esq.; it was the first fight he was ever in, and he was so taken up with it that he's had a permanent black eye ever since."


CHAPTER XVI

SECRET SIGNS

"You can find lots of ways of makin' money honestly besides workin' for it, especially if you read the newspapers," said Private Smith, who by the way has been taking part in "skeleton" manoeuvres, when pieces of paper stuck on a stick were supposed to represent impregnable positions, and three men and a drummer-boy stood for an army corps. Smithy is very pleased with himself for he has been representing in turn—

A brigade of infantry,

A quick-firing gun,

A convoy.

and the only occurrence that has clouded his joy was his unfortunate meeting (whilst he was pretending to be an infantry brigade) with the balloon section of the enemy (represented by Private "Swop" Taylor, of the Wessex Regiment).

The irate umpire who found the balloon section and the infantry brigade fast asleep by the side of a common lunch had first sworn, then threatened, then laughed, for he was an umpire with a sense of humour, and really ought not to have been an umpire at all.

"Some fellers," said Private Smith, "learn a lot from things that appear in newspapers.

"We used to have a chap in 'B' Company who was a rare one for finding out how many shillin's put end to end would reach from here to there, so to speak. 'Suppose you dug a hole straight down through the earth, where would you come out?' he sez.

"'The other end,' sez Nobby Clark, which was quite true.

"Well, this feller—name of Bertie—was full of information that nobody wanted to know, an' from what I've heard he got it all out of newspapers. The only feller who was interested was Nobby Clark, an' Nobby used to get Bertie to tell him things by the hour—such as the curious marriage customs of the South Sea Islands, how many pints of water there was in the North Sea or German Ocean, the number of left-handed people in
Ireland, and that sort of thing.

"Bit by bit the thing sort of grew on Nobby, for he was always a bit interested in newspapers. You see, Nobby is one of those fellers who are always writin' for samples. If he sees an advertisement in the newspaper sayin' 'Send a post card for a sample tin,' he ups an' borrows a post card from some young chap who don't know him well enough to refuse, and before you know where you are, back comes the sample tin with a long letter showin' you how much of the cocoa turns into fat, how much into bone, etcetera.

"Nobby gets a big boxful of things, an' when he's short of cash he sells 'em off to the troops. Bottles of the stuff that the butcher shocks so, tins of cocoa, cards of pen nibs, bottles of nerve pills, stuff for making your hair grow, and any number of books about the Encyclo—what-d'ye-call-it?

There was one advertisement about a new language—what's the name of it again? Yes that's it. Esperanto. Accordin' to the book Nobby got, it was the sort of language everybody would talk if there wasn't any other language. Well, Nobby was very struck on it, and used to go about Esperanting. One day the orderly sergeant came in to tell Nobby he was for guard. 'Moodgy-koodgy,' sez Nobby—it sounded like that, anyway—and Nobby was put into the guard-room for swearing at his superior officer.

"Nobby explained himself next day an' got let off with a caution.

"'No more bloomin' Esperanto for me,' sez Nobby; 'I'm goin' to stick to fit cures an' bakin' powders,' he sez. 'Wot's the good of learnin' a language when there ain't no country to talk it in?'

"But somehow the Esper gave Nobby an idea, and a few days later he come to me an' borrows a shilling. I never mind lendin' money to Nobby, because he's very honest about money matters, and I know he'd pay me back if he had to steal it."

Smithy was silent for a moment, then—

"Have you ever heard tell of Every Lover's Code and Sign Book? No? Well, no more hadn't I; but Nobby saw the advertisement in a young lady's paper that he reads every week, so he wrote for a sample.

"The Code and Sign Company sent back a little handbill showin' how you can tell a young lady you love her by drawin' the first finger of the right hand down the side of your nose, an' certain other signs for 'We are observed,' an' 'Not to-night, but some other night,' an' 'Beware of the dark man.'

This pleased Nobby so much that he borrowed the money from me an' a stamp from another chap an' got the book, an' from the very first day he had that book Nobby made money out of it.

"It happens there was lots of chaps in barracks who knew girls by sight an' wanted to be introduced to 'em, but hadn't the nerve to walk up to 'em in a society way and say, 'Fine evenin', miss; what do you say to a stroll?'

"When Nobby explained that all the young ladies in town knew the book by heart, the chaps wanted to buy the book, but Nobby said that was a silly waste of money, an' he offered to teach the signs at the rate of six a penny.

"Nobby used to have a little class of a couple of dozen chaps down in the cricket field, and I used to collect the money whilst Nobby talked. Somehow, these meetin's turned into a sort of secret society. It was Nobby's idea, an' we had a pass-word, and Nobby was secretary and treasurer, an' we used to call each other 'brother.'

"There was one sign that Nobby was very particular about, an' that was the 'comrade-in-distress' sign. When you saw a feller rubbin' the back of his head very fierce it meant 'Lend me fourpence, an' I will pay you to-morrow.'

"Spud Murphy asked if that little bit was in the book, an' Nobby said yes, but when Spud asked to see the book Nobby said that was against the rules. Anyhow, if it was in the book it didn't seem to work, an' me an' Nobby wore a bald place in the backs of our heads one afternoon tryin' it.

"'Why didn't you answer my sign?' he said to Spud Murphy that night.

"'What sign, brother?' sez Spud, surprised.

"'The "comrade-in-distress" sign,' sez Nobby.

"'Good gracious!' sez Spud, or words to that effect, 'I thought that was the "I-have-loved-you-for-years" sign!'

"Nobby's idea in the secret society was that all the chaps was to club together an' pay tuppence a week, an' if any one of the brothers got into trouble the money was to go to bail him out, or buy him a weddin' gift or somethin' of that sort. Nobby was treasurer—I told you that before. Nobby drew up a list of the things you could draw compensation for. Struck by lightnin' was one; fallin' out of a balloon was another; bein' blown up on a motor-car was another. I can't remember the full list, but I know you could only get your money back if something happened that wasn't likely to happen once in a thousand years, and when Spud Murphy got fined by the Colonel seven-and-sixpence for riotous conduct owing to his uncle coming down to see him and paying for the drink, Nobby said the fine couldn't be paid out of the society's funds.

"'For why' sez Spud.

"'Because,' sez Nobby, the rules say—

"'Wasn't it an accident?' sez Spud fiercely.

"'No,' sez Nobby, 'it was natural causes.'

"The secret society got into a bit of discredit soon after that owing to Happy Johnson, who's a very absentminded chap, meetin' the Colonel on High Street, and givin' him the 'let-us-part-friends' sign instead of the salute.

"When Happy came out of cells he said he'd been thinkin' things over, an' decided that the society wasn't all it was cracked up to be, an' he asked Nobby to call a meetin'. Nobby said certainly, so the brothers all met in the cricket field by the side of the river, and Happy moved that the society be broken up and that all the brothers get their money back.

"It was rather a slack time, toward the end of the month, and most of the brothers said 'Hear, hear.'

"Then Spud made a speech, and a feller in 'H' company made a speech, and a chap named Williams, who's got an uncle who was a guardian till they found him out, he made a speech, and everybody said the same thing, that the society was a rotten one and they wanted their money back.

"Nobby saw that something was goin' to happen, but for the life of him he couldn't think out a sign to give in reply to the rude remarks of his brethren. There he stood, as cool as a cucumber, listening to what they had to say.

"At the end of it all Nobby replied. I tell you," said Smithy enthusiastically, "Nobby looked fine. He wore a bit of blue ribbon round his neck to show he was the treasurer and secretary, although most of the fellers knew it, owing to Nobby drawing their tuppences every week.

"'Dear brothers,' sez Nobby sadly, 'the red-haired thief brother who has just spoke, an' the wall-eyed liar brother who spoke before, sez the secret society must be broke up. Well, it's broke up,' an' he sorrowfully took the blue ribbon from his neck and put it in his trousers pocket, an' commenced to walk away.

"''Ere!' sez Spud Murphy, 'what about the money?'

"'What money?' sez Nobby, surprised.

"'We want our tuppences back,' sez Spud. An' the other fellers said, 'Hear, hear.'

"Nobby thought a bit, then—

"'Give me the "want-my-money-back" sign' he set firmly.

That upset Spud.

"'Why—why,' he sez, bewildered, 'there ain't any such sign—you haven't taught it.'

"Nobby smiled sadly.

"'No, I know I haven't. I was goin' to teach you that sign next week; but the society's broke up, an' You'll never know that sign,' he sez, and walked away."

CHAPTER XVII

THE FAITH OF PRIVATE SIMPSON

*This story has the disadvantage of being a true story—"disadvantage" because true stories are always dull. I vouch for the truth, because I was with Private Simpson at the moment of his passing. I remember the night as if it were yesterday. The dark tent, and the flickering candle, and the straw on the floor of the fluttering marquee. I remember it well, and I wish you could have seen it—you who have contributed your money towards justifying the faith of Private Simpson. —E.W.]*

"You quite understand," said Private Smith, of the 1st Anchester Regiment, "that it took us a long time before we got the hang of this here Union Jack Club.

"The Army is full up of soldiers' institutes, and the places where soldiers can get a Bright 'Arf Hour, an' one or two more or less don't make much difference.

"But when me or Nobby get an invitation to a Bright 'Arf Hour we always read the bill through to see if hymn books are provided, an' if they are, we don't go—see?"

Smithy was in a hurry to explain.

"Don't think it's because me an' Nobby are down on religious tea-fights an' bun struggles because they're religious, because you'll be fallin' over yourself. I take my religion with the band on Sunday mornin'—parade at 10.30 in church parade kit, an' march away, to the admiration of the town. 'A' company bein' the first company on parade, an' the first to march into church, we're nearer the pulpit, so, in a manner of speakin', we get more religion than the other fellers.

"But the mistake that people make is that you can't do good work without a hymn book, and that's where the 'soldiers' home' business goes to pot.

## ON SOLDIERS' HOMES

"Soldiers don't like bein' rescued all the time; they don't like bein' saved from theirselves, an' that's why you find 'soldiers' clubs' never do the same roarin' business as 'The Artillery Arms.' A lot of people run away with the idea that he's a desperate character. They have special meetin's for him, an' likely as not they get up a subscription an build a home with a bagatelle board and an 'armonium to keep him out of the nice, comfortable public houses.

"An' there's meetin' of the Young Soldiers Botanical Class on Wednesdays, an a choir practice on Thursdays an the temperance section has a meetin' on Fridays, and there's an enjoyable Sankey sing-song on Saturdays, an' coffee is provided at moderate prices.

"There was a chap of oure named Simpson—Snark Simpson of 'A'. He used to go in for politics; before he joined the Army he was a waiter at the Deptford Liberal Club, and what he didn't know about Gladstone wasn't worth knowin'. He was aiways grousin' about things—about the Army, an' the officers, and how it ought to be run. He was down on soldiers' clubs, because he'd got a funny idea that a feller could be good without singin' hymns. But mostly bis grumblin' took the form of sayin' 'What's the good?' Sometimes we called him 'What's-the-good Simpson,' an' it used to be quite a sayin' in 'A' Company, 'What's the good?'

## WHY SIMPSON LAUGHED

"When all the papers was full of the Dargai business, an' people at music-halls was singin' about the 'Gallant Gordons on the Dargai Heights,' old Simpson used to laugh an' sneer till me an' Nobby nearly hit him.

"'That's all right,' he sez, laughin', 'but what's the good of fellers chuckin' their lives away? People will forget all about it by Derby Day, an' if one of them gallant Highlanders goes into a private bar an' asks for a drink for a hero, the girl behind the counter will tell him that they keep a special bar for 'eroes—the bottle an' jug department.'

"'Well, old Simpson went on, an' went on, sneerin' an' grousin', an' said that if he ever had to choose between bein' a one-legged 'ero an' a two-legged shirker, he knew what he'd do.

"The war broke out, an' we was sent from Malta to the Orange Free State. We had one or two little fights, but nothin' to speak of.

"One mornin' Nobby sez to me, 'Smithy,' he sez, quits grave, 'there's goin' to be a big scrap to-day. I heard old Umfreville say so. I wish you'd keep your eye on Snarky Simpson. I don't want him to show up the company. As like as not he'll bolt.

"It started at daybreak an' went on till the afternoon. We got in a tight corner with four pom-poms playin' on the regiment. We sat tight for six hours, an' then advanced against the kopje where the Boers was. You'd hear fellers squeal like rabbits an' go spinnin' round an' drop, an' the regiment was absolutely white to a man—but we kept advancin'.

"WHAT'S THE GOOD—?"

"I kept my eye on Simpson, but he didn't look worse than any of the others. Then we charged—we charged a hill, an' we got half-way up when the Boers opened out on us. Ten men in my section went down. Two of the officers dropped. Poor little Captain Grey... a horrible sight. The fire was worse than you can think of. The regiment stopped an' sort of hesitated—but Simpson didn't stop; I can see him now, with his bayonet fixed an' his khaki helmet on the back of his bead, stumblin' along over the loose stones. He didn't seem to realise be was advancin' alone, an' when he did, he stopped an' looked back. Then, above all the cracklin' an' tick-tookin' of the rifles, you could hear his voice: 'Come on, you blighters. What's the good...?'

"We laughed, yes, we actually laughed, an' then the company rushed forward, scramblin' over the rocks an' firin' steady at every chance. It was Nobby who caught hold of Simpson just as he was fallin'.

"'Hold up.' sez Nobby.

"'What's the good?' sez Simpson, talkin' like a man in his sleep; an' we laid him down.

"Then the grass on the bill caught fire, an' the medical staff worked like devils to get the wounded out before they was burned. Yes," said Smithy, seriously, "the old Linseed Lancers were heroes that day, an' I forgive them for all their sins. They came out black an' scorched, draggin' the wounded with 'em, but me an' Nobby brought old Simpson out. We got him down to the field hospital an' into the marquee. There was lots of chaps laid flat that day, an' it was nearly nine o'clock that night before the doctor could see old Simpson.

UNDERSTANDING

"Me an' Nobby was sittin' with him when the doctor came. Nobby was was holdin' his hand, an'—an' I—"

I waited.

"I was readin' to him," said Smithy, quietly, 'a-readin' a bit of the Bible. The doctor looked at Simpson an' said gently:

"'You're badly hit, Simpson.'

"'Am I dyin'?' said Simpson.

"The doctor nodded his head, an' by an' by went away.

"Simpson lay for a long time an' said nothing; then after a bit he said:

"'Smithy, I know what's the good now,' be said.

"'What about?' I asked him.

"'About soldiers dyin' in action. Why,' he said, 'if chaps like me an' you didn't die, nobody would take any notice of them that live—don't you see, Smithy? Civilians'll think a lot more of soldiers because chaps like me...' He stopped, but Nobby and me understood.

"At four o'clock in the mornin' he asked for a drink, an' then he said:

"'What's that?'

"It was firing—the pickets were engaged, an' there was a little fight going on: so we told him.

"He smiled a little.

"'Perhaps them chaps are wonderin' what's the good, too,' he said, an' shut his eyes. I think Nobby was cryin', because he was very fond of Simpson.

"When he opened his eyes again he said, 'The people at home will think a lot of us...' An' then I heard the regimental assembly go, an' knew the Anchesters was falling in.

"'We've got to leave you now, old feller,' sez Nobby. But Simpson took no notice, because he was dead.

## Edgar Wallace – A Short Biography

Richard Horatio Edgar Wallace was born on the 1st April 1875 at 7 Ashburnham Grove, Greenwich. His mother, Mary Jane "Polly" Richards was born into an Irish Catholic family in Liverpool in 1843 and had worked in theatres, both as an actress in bit-parts and as a stagehand and usherette, until she married a Merchant Navy Captain, Joseph Richards, in 1867. He too had been born into an Irish Catholic family in Liverpool. His father had also been a Captain in the Merchant Navy, and his mother's family had a marine background. Mary was eight months pregnant with Joseph's child when he died at sea, and it was once the child had been born that she first turned to the stage, taking the stage name Polly Richards.

She joined the Marriott family theatre troupe in 1872. It was managed by Mrs. Alice Edgar, Richard Edgar, Grace Edgar, Adeline Edgar and Richard Horatio Edgar, Wallace's father. In late 1874 Mary and Richard Horatio Edgar had a brief sexual encounter at the party following a successful show, and she fell pregnant. Worried about the scandal which would ensue and fearing that she might forever lose her job at the troupe, she fabricated an obligation in Greenwich would detain her there for at least six months. She lived in a room in the boarding house on Ashburnham Grove until her son, Edgar, was born. She had already made preparations through her midwife for a couple to foster the child, and when Edgar was born the midwife presented her with Mrs Freeman. Her husband was a fishmonger at Billingsgate market and she already had ten children. She was happy to foster the child and for Polly to make frequent visits to see him in exchange for a small sum of money which Polly made from her work n the theatre troupe.

Wallace was now known as Richard Horatio Edgar Freeman, taking his father's forenames and his foster family's surname. Broadly speaking his childhood was a happy one. The Freemans looked after him lovingly and he had good friendships with his foster siblings, particularly Clara Freeman, twenty years his senior, who often looked after him as a child. After a few years Polly's finances tightened and she was no longer in a position to afford the fee she had been paying the Freemans. However, they had grown to love the young Wallace and opted to adopt him in order to keep him out of the workhouse. Polly could no longer visit him. George Freeman was keen to ensure that he had equal opportunities and did all he could to secure him an education at St. Alfege with St. Peter's, a Peckham boarding school. Despite his adoptive father's efforts, though, Wallace left the school aged twelve for truancy.

Instead he went to work and by the time he was fourteen or fifteen he had experience selling newspapers at Ludgate Circus, near Fleet Street, as a worker in a rubber factory, as a shoe shop assistant, as a milk delivery boy and as a ship's cook. He stole from the milk company which resulted in his dismissal, and in 1894 was engaged to a local girl from Deptford named Edith Anstree, though he broke this off and instead joined the Infantry. He adopted the name Edgar Wallace which he took from Lew Wallace, the author of *Ben-Hur*, and his medical record records a diminutive 33" chest and a stunted growth. his first posting was with the West Kent Regiment in South Africa in 1896, though he did not enjoy military life, arranging to be transferred to the Royal Army Medical Corps. Though this was a less strenuous job, it was also significantly less pleasant and so he again transferred to the Press Corps, which he found suited him far better.

He was in Cape Town in 1898 where he met Rudyard Kipling and was inspired to begin writing and publishing poetry and songs. His first collection of ballads, *The Mission that Failed!* and was enough of a success that in 1899 he paid his way out of the armed forces in order to turn to writing full time. His first work was as a war correspondent for Reuters who kept him in Africa to cover the Boer War, and then for the Daily Mail in 1900 and various other periodicals after that. It was while he was in South Africa that he met and married Ivy Maude Caldecott, who was 21 when they married in 1901, despite her Wesleyan missionary father's strong opposition to the union, for several reasons, one of which was that Wallace's writing was not turning quite the profit he had expected it would. *War and Other Poems* and *Writ in Barracks,* both published in 1900, had not proved as popular as his first collection. Eleanor Clare Hellier Wallace, their first child, died of meningitis in 1903 and, in rather deep debt, they returned to London. Wallace used his contacts with the Daily Mail to get work with them in London, electing to write detective novels as a means of making quick money.

Wallace met Polly, his birth mother, in 1903. He didn't remember her from his childhood as he had been too young when she became unable to visit, so it was as though they were meeting for the first time. She was sixty years old and terminally ill, living in abject poverty. She had come to Wallace seeking financial support, but he turned her away. She died in the Bradford Infirmary later that year. In 1904 he and Ivy had a son, Bryan. He was still writing and had completed his first thriller, *The Four Just Men*. Since nobody would publish it he resorted to setting up his own publishing company which he called Tallis Press and he published a serialised version of *The Four Just Men* in 1905. He received promotional assistance from the Daily Mail in which he ran a competition for entrants to guess the method of murder in the final chapter, with a prize of £1,000 for a correct guess. Although the paper's proprietor, Lord Alfred Harmsworth, refused Wallace the £1,000 prize money, Wallace persisted and went ahead with the competition, recklessly advertising on billboards and buses all over the country, hoping to expand his advertisements across the Empire. His worried colleagues at the Daily Mail managed to convince him to lower the prize money to £500, split into a first prize of £250, a second prize of £200 and a third of

£50, but with the total cost of his advertisements nearing £2,000 he would need to sell £2,500 worth of copies before he could see any profit. He was confident that this could be achieved in just three months.

Though he had remarkable enthusiasm, it became clear that his managerial skills left a lot to be desired. It soon emerged that nowhere in the competition terms and conditions had he included a clause limiting the competition to one single winner; instead, any entrant with a winning answer was entitled to their corresponding prize money. Thus, if ten entrants guessed the first prize answer, the competition was obliged to pay each entrant £250. This error was only noticed after the competition had been closed and the solution had been printed in the final installment of the novel, meaning that not only was there no opportunity to write his way out of enormous financial obligation, but the entrants who had guessed correctly would by now have read the final chapter and know they had done so. £250 was an enormous amount of money to the average Edwardian family and those entitled to it were likely to make a lot of noise if they didn't receive their money. Despite this, Wallace's fist instinct was to attempt to ignore the issue entirely, even as he discovered that he initial calculations had been dramatically over-enthusiastic and it would take nearer to two years of continuous sales to break even at the initial cost of £2,500, let alone the new figure which included every correct guesser. Compounding the problem even further was the awful realisation that as sales continued throughout the initial three month period and Wallace approached the £2,500 break-even figure, new readers were still eligible to enter and guess correctly. Though it is unknown how much he eventually owed his readers, Lord Harmsworth found himself having to loan over £5,000 in order to protect the reputation of the newspaper, since 1906 had come around and there still hadn't been a list printed of all prize-winners. It was less a charitable act than one of a man anxious that the failure would reflect ill on his own paper. Wallace filed for bankruptcy shortly thereafter and as a token gesture to his creditors sold the rights to the novel to Sir George Newnes, a publisher and editor, for £75. In the midst of this chaos though, Wallace managed to write and published *Smithy*, which would become the first of a series of *Smithy* novels.

Following this fiascos Wallace was dismissed from the Daily Mail in 1907 when inaccuracies which were found in his reporting, resulting in libel cases being brought against the paper. That year he became the first reporter to be fired from the Daily Mail and was his awful reputation prevented him from finding work at any other papers. Despite all this, though, he travelled to the Congo Free State later that year and reported on the criminal treatment of the Congolese people by King Leopold II of Belgium and the Belgian rubber companies. Up to fifteen million Congolese were killed in various atrocities, and Wallace was asked to serialise stories based on his experiences for her penny magazine *Weekly Tale-Teller*. He and Ivy had another daughter, named Patricia, in 1908. Though his new work for *Weekly Tale-Teller* was bringing in some money, their financial situation was still dire and Ivy was occasionally forced to sell off her jewellery and possessions in order to pay for food. In 1911 his Congolese stories were published in a collection called *Sanders of the River*, which quickly became a bestseller. He would publish eleven more such collections featuring a total of 102 stories of adventure and tribal life set on the river Congo.

From 1908 he started to enjoy a revival of both his success and his reputation. The majority of his initial writing he sold outright in order to make money as quickly as possible and placate his creditors in the United Kingdom and South Africa, but as his success saw the reestablishment of his reputation he began to find work once again as a journalist, beginning in horse racing for the *Week-End*, the *Evening News* and then as an editor for the *Week-End Racing Supplement*. Following this success he started his own racing papers, *Bibury's* and *R. E. Walton's Weekly*, eventually buying his own racehorses and losing thousands gambling. His success was insufficient to support his newly extravagant lifestyle and his marriage began to fail in the light of his financial irresponsibility. He and Ivy had their last child together,

Michael Blair Wallace, in 1916, and she filed for divorce in 1918 moving to Tunbridge Wells with her children.

Wallace began to fall for his secretary Ethel Violet King and they married in 1921, having a child, Penelope Wallace, in 1923, who would herself go on to become a successful crime writer. Wallace now began to take his career as a fiction writer more seriously, signing with Hodder and Stoughton in 1921. He now began to organize his contracts more carefully, arranging for royalties and properly organized promotions, run by people more business-minded than himself. He was marketed as the 'King of Thrillers' and they gave him the trademark image of a trilby, a cigarette holder and a yellow Rolls Royce. He was truly prolific, capable not only of producing a 70,000 word novel in three days but of doing three novels in a row in such a manner. His publishers signed off on almost everything he wrote as soon as he turned it in, estimating that by 1928 one in four books being read at any time was written by Wallace, for alongside his famous thrillers he wrote variously in other genres, including but not limited to science fiction, non-fiction accounts of WWI which amounted to ten volumes and screen plays. Eventually he would reach the remarkable total of 170 novels, 18 stage plays and 957 short stories.

Wallace became chairman of the Press Club which to this day holds an annual Edgar Wallace Award, rewarding 'excellence in writing'. In 1923 he broadcasted a report on the Epsom Derby horse race for the British Broadcasting Company, making him the first ever radio sports correspondent. His ex-wife Ivy had suffered from breast cancer between 1923-1924, and it eventually killed her in 1926 despite a successful operation to remove a tumour the year before. He wrote the essay "The Canker in our Midst" in 1926 which dealt, aggressively and controversially, with the problem of paedophilia in show business, describing how children were unwittingly left open to sexual abuse, and linking paedophilia with homosexuality. Its tone has been described as "intolerant, blustering, kick-the-blighters-down-the-stairs". He was appointed chairman of the British Lion Film Corporation on the back of the success of *The Ringer* and on the agreement that he give British Lion first choice on all his future work. This contract gave him an annual salary and a large amount of stock with the company, along with a stipend on all British Lion production of his work and 10% of their annual profits. This extraordinary contract gave him annual earnings by 1929 of almost £50,000, or almost £2 million in 2014.

He now became an active figure in politics, entering the 1931 general election as a Liberal contestant in Blackpool, rejecting the current government in favour of free trade. He lost the election by over 33,000 votes and went to America in late 1931, once again deeply in debt after buying the *Sunday News* which closed six months later. In America he quickly found work as a script doctor for RKO Pictures, enjoying early success with the 1932 adaptation of *The Hound of the Baskervilles*. This success, along with that of the play *The Green Pack*, established his reputation in America and he was able to see his own work adapted for film, beginning with *The Four Just Men*. His most successful theatrical work, *On The Spot*, which explores the life of Al Capone, has been described as "arguably, in construction, dialogue, action, plot and resolution, still one of the finest and purest of 20th-century melodramas". These successes led to his assignation on RKO's "gorilla picture" which would become famous as King Kong in 1933.

He worked on the first draft though he was beginning to experience severe headaches which brought about a diagnosis of diabetes. Despite taking medication to address his condition, it deteriorated in a matter of days. His wife booked him passage home but soon heard that he had entered a coma and died of his condition and double pneumonia on the 7th of February 1932 in North Maple Drive, Beverly Hills. In his honour the bell at St. Bride's church on Fleet Street tolled for the duration of the morning while the flags flew at half-mast. He was buried near his home in England at Chalklands, Bourne End, in Buckinghamshire. Once again, at the time of his death he was in severe debt, mostly to racing bookkeepers, though these debts were settled within two years thanks to the enormous royalties his estate continued to receive from his contracts. His writing has been translated into 29 languages, and is considered one of the most important bodies of Colonial writing.

Edgar Wallace – A Concise Bibliography

**African Novels**
Sanders of the River (1911)
The People of the River (1911)
The River of Stars (1913)
Bosambo of the River (1914)
Bones (1915)
The Keepers of the King's Peace (1917)
Lieutenant Bones (1918)
Bones in London (1921)
Sandi the Kingmaker (1922)
Bones of the River (1923)
Sanders (1926)
Again Sanders (1928)

**Four Just Men (Series)**
The Four Just Men (1905)
The Council of Justice (1908)
The Just Men of Cordova (1917)
The Law of the Four Just Men (US title: Again the Three Just Men) (1921)
The Three Just Men (1926)
Again the Three Just Men (US title: The Law of the Three Just Men) (1929) a.k.a. Again the Three

**Mr. J. G. Reeder (Series)**
Room 13 (1924)
The Mind of Mr. J. G. Reeder (US title: The Murder Book of Mr. J. G. Reeder) (1925)
Terror Keep (1927)
Red Aces (1929)[27]
The Guv'nor and Other Short Stories (US title: Mr. Reeder Returns) (1932)

**Detective Sgt. (Inspector) Elk series**
The Nine Bears or The Other Man or The Cheaters (1910)
revised as Silinski - Master Criminal (1930)
The Fellowship of the Frog (1925)
The Joker or The Colossus (1926)
The Twister (1928)
The India-Rubber Men (1929)
White Face (1930)

**Educated Evans (Series)**
Educated Evans (1924)
More Educated Evans (1926)

Good Evans (1927)

**Smithy (Series)**
Smithy (1905)
Smithy Abroad (1909)
Smithy and The Hun (1915)
Nobby or Smithy's Friend Nobby (1916)

**Crime Novels**
Angel Esquire (1908)
The Fourth Plague or Red Hand (1913)
Grey Timothy or Pallard the Punter (1913)
The Man Who Bought London (1915)
The Melody of Death (1915)
A Debt Discharged (1916)
The Tomb of T'Sin (1916)
The Secret House (1917)
The Clue of the Twisted Candle (1918)
Down under Donovan (1918)
The Man Who Knew (1918)
The Strange Lapses of Larry Loman (1918)
The Green Rust (1919)
Kate Plus Ten (1919)
The Daffodil Mystery or The Daffodil Murder (1920)
Jack O'Judgment (1920)
The Angel of Terror or The Destroying Angel (1922)
The Crimson Circle (1922)
Mr. Justice Maxwell or Take-A-Chance Anderson( 1922)
The Valley of Ghosts (1922)
Captains of Souls (1923)
The Clue of the New Pin (1923)
The Green Archer (1923)
The Missing Million (1923)
The Dark Eyes of London or The Croakers (1924)
Double Dan or Diana of Kara-Kara (US Title) (1924)
The Face in the Night or The Diamond Men or The Ragged Princess (1924)
The Sinister Man (1924)
The Three Oak Mystery (1924)
The Blue Hand or Beyond Recall (1925)
The Daughters of the Night (1925)
The Gaunt Stranger or Police Work (1925) revised as The Ringer (1926)
A King by Night (1925)
The Strange Countess (1925)
The Avenger or The Hairy Arm (1926)
'The Black Abbot (1926)
The Day of Uniting (1926)
The Door with Seven Locks (1926)
The Man from Morocco or Souls In Shadows or The Black (US Title) (1926)

The Million Dollar Story (1926)
The Northing Tramp or The Tramp (1926)
Penelope of the Polyantha (1926)
The Square Emerald or The Woman (1926)
The Terrible People or The Gallows' Hand (1926)
We Shall See! or The Gaol-Breakers (US Title) (1926)
The Yellow Snake or The Black Tenth (1926)
Big Foot (1927)
The Feathered Serpent or Inspector Wade or Inspector Wade and the Feathered Serpent (1927)
Flat 2 (1927)
The Forger or The Counterfeiter (1927)
Terror Keep (1927)
The Hand of Power or The Proud Sons of Ragusa (1927)
The Man Who Was Nobody (1927)
Number Six (1927)
The Squeaker or The Sign of the Leopard or The Squealer (US Title) (1927)
The Traitor's Gate (1927)
The Double (1928)
The Flying Squad (1928)
The Gunner or Gunman's Bluff (US Title) (1928)
Four Square Jane or The Fourth Square (1929)
The Golden Hades or Stamped In Gold or The Sinister Yellow Sign (1929)
The Green Ribbon (1929)
The Calendar (1930)
The Clue of the Silver Key or The Silver Key (1930)
The Lady of Ascot (1930)
The Devil Man or Sinister Street or Silver Steel
or The Life and Death of Charles Peace (1931)
The Man at the Carlton or The Mystery of Mary Grier (1931)
The Coat of Arms or The Arranways Mystery (1931)
On the Spot: Violence and Murder in Chicago (1931)
When the Gangs Came to London or Scotland Yard's Yankee Dick
or The Gangsters Come To London (1932)
The Frightened Lady or The Case of the Frightened Lady or Criminal At Large (1933)
The Green Pack (1933)
The Man Who Changed His Name (1935)
The Mouthpiece (1935)
Smoky Cell (1935)
The Table (1936)
Sanctuary Island (1936)

**Other Novels**
Captain Tatham of Tatham Island or Eve's Island or The Island of Galloping Gold (1909)
The Duke in the Suburbs (1909)
Private Selby (1912)
"1925" - The Story of a Fatal Peace (1915)
Those Folk of Bulboro (1918)
The Book of all Power (1921)

Flying Fifty-five (1922)
The Books of Bart (1923)
Barbara on Her Own (1926)

**Poetry Collections**
The Mission That Failed (1898)
War and Other Poems (1900)
Writ In Barracks (1900)

**Non-Fiction**
Unofficial Despatches of the Anglo-Boer War (1901)
Famous Scottish Regiments (1914)
Field Marshal Sir John French (1914)
Heroes All: Gallant Deeds of the War (1914)
The Standard History of the War – Volumes 1 – 4 (1914)
Kitchener's Army and the Territorial Forces:
The Full Story of a Great Achievement (1915)
Vol. 2-4. War of the Nations (1915)
Vol. 5-7. War of the Nations (1916)
Vol. 8-9. War of the Nations (1917)
Famous Men and Battles of the British Empire (1917)
Tam of the Scouts (1918)
The Real Shell-Man: The Story of Chetwynd of Chilwell (1919)
People or Edgar Wallace by Himself(1926)
The Trial of Patrick Herbert Mahon (1928)
My Hollywood Diary (1932)

**Screenplays**
King Kong (1932, first draft of original screenplay, 110 pages) While the script was not used in its
entirety, much of it was retained for the final screenplay.
The Hound of the Baskervilles (1932, British film)
The Squeaker (1930, British film)
Prince Gabby (1929, British film)
Mark of the Frog (1928, American film)
The Valley of Ghosts (192

**Short Story Collections**
The Admirable Carfew (1914)
The Adventure of Heine (1917)
Tam O' the Scouts (1918)
The Fighting Scouts (1919)
Chick (1923)
The Black Avons (1925)
The Brigand (1927)
The Mixer (1927)
This England (1927)
The Orator (1928)
The Thief in the Night (1928)

Elegant Edward (1928)
The Lone House Mystery and Other Stories (1929)
The Governor of Chi-Foo (1929)
Again the Ringer The Ringer Returns (US Title) (1929)
The Big Four or Crooks of Society (1929)
The Black or Blackmailers I Have Foiled (1929)
The Cat-Burglar (1929)
Circumstantial Evidence (1929)
Fighting Snub Reilly (1929)
For Information Received (1929)
Forty-Eight Short Stories (1929)
Planetoid 127 and The Sweizer Pump (1929)
The Ghost of Down Hill & The Queen of Sheba's Belt (1929)
The Iron Grip (1929)
The Lady of Little Hell (1929)
The Little Green Man (1929)
The Prison-Breakers (1929)
The Reporter (1929)
Killer Kay (1930)
Mrs William Jones and Bill (1930)
Forty Eight Short-Stories (1930)
The Stretelli Case and Other Mystery Stories (1930)
The Terror (1930)
The Lady Called Nita (1930)
Sergeant Sir Peter or Sergeant Dunn, C.I.D. (1932)
The Scotland Yard Book of Edgar Wallace (1932)
The Steward (1932)
Nig-Nog and other humorous stories (1934)
The Last Adventure (1934)
The Woman From the East (1934) Co-written By Robert George Curtis
The Edgar Wallace Reader of Mystery and Adventure (1943)
The Undisclosed Client (1963)

**Other**
King Kong, with Draycott M. Dell, (1933), 28 October 1933 Cinema Weekly

**Plays**
An African Millionaire (1904)
The Forest of Happy Dreams (1910)
Dolly Cutting Herself (1911)
The Manager's Dream (1914)
M'Lady (1921)
Double Dan (1926)
The Mystery of room 45 (1926)
A Perfect Gentleman (1927)
The Terror (1927)
Traitors Gate (1927)
The Lad (1928)

The Man Who Changed His Name (1928)
The Squeaker (1928)
The Calendar (1929)
Persons Unknown (1929)
The Ringer (1929)
The Mouthpiece (1930)
On the Spot (1930)
Smoky Cell (1930)
The Squeaker (1930)
To Oblige A Lady (1930)
The Case of the Frightened Lady (1931)
The Old Man (1931)
The Green Pack (1932)
The Table (1932)

www.ingramcontent.com/pod-product-compliance
Lightning Source LLC
Chambersburg PA
CBHW071411170626
46811CB00003B/1360